A GAME TWO COULD PLAY

Belinda knew she should have been suspicious when her husband, Lord Gerald Courtenay, commissioned the handsome Chrétien d'Angoulême to paint her portrait. Now the truth was out. Chrétien was to keep her occupied while her husband enjoyed the charms of the mistress he clearly preferred to her.

This left Belinda with a choice of either throwing herself into the arms of the libertine Lord Furneaux, whom she long had adored from afar—or accepting the *amour* of the captivating Chrétien.

One thing was sure. Revenge would be sweet—if not quite safe. . . .

ELLEN FITZGERALD is a pseudonym for a well-known romance writer. A graduate of the University of Southern California with a B.A. in English and an M.A. in Drama, Ms. Fitzgerald has also attended Yale University and has had numerous plays produced throughout the country. In her spare time, she designs and sells jewelry. Ms. Fitzgerald lives in New York City.

An Unwelcome Alliance

Ellen Fitzgerald

A SIGNET BOOK

NEW AMERICAN LIBRARY

1

" 'The uneven, stone-strewn road wound upward, ever upward. On one side, jagged cliffs towered over a dark and sullen stream of water—' "

"Stop, please," Lady Cornelia Hazzard, a lissome blond of some nineteen summers, protested. She turned large puzzled gray eyes on the face of Lady Belinda Devereux, who was currently reading out loud from her own manuscript, a novel-in-progress tentatively entitled *Lady Cassandra's Secret.*

"Well?" Cornelia received a smoldering green glance from the author. Sticking her finger between the closely written sheets of foolscap to mark her place, she inquired in acerbic tones,

"What is the matter, pray?"

"I am very sorry to interrupt you, Belinda, but I feel that I must question you on your use of the adjective 'sullen.' "

"And why, pray, would you do that?" the author demanded belligerently.

"My dear, how can a *stream* be sullen? I

could understand 'sluggish' or 'slow,' but *sullen*? It is not as if bodies of water possessed *human* feelings."

With pardonable annoyance, Belinda said, "I *meant* slow-moving. And if Milton can use it, so can I. This couplet is from *Il Penseroso*. I will repeat it for your edification, Cornelia:

" 'Oft, on a plat of rising ground.
     I hear the far-off curfew sound.
   Over some wide-watered shore,
   Swinging low with sullen roar.'

"I presume that a curfew is a bell, though it is sometimes very hard to guess just what poets really mean. Still, I suspect that he meant a bell, and if a bell can *sound* sullen, a stream can certainly look sullen. Do you wish to hear more of my novel or would you rather not? It was you who suggested that I read it to you."

"Oh, I certainly do wish to hear more," Cornelia said eagerly. "I am enjoying this novel even more than your last one."

"You are?" The author sounded less gratified than challenging. "Was my other one so ill-conceived, then?"

"Oh, no, Belinda, gracious, how you do take one up!" Cornelia sighed. "I liked *The Maltravers Curse*. In fact, I think it ought to be published. I hope that they can both be published. Please go on reading."

"I do not want any more interruptions," Belinda adjured her.

"I swear that I will be as silent as the grave," Cornelia said solemnly.

"Please," Belinda begged. Then she giggled.

"Now you are sounding gothic. Perhaps you ought to try your hand at a novel, Cornelia."

"I wish I could, but I do not have your talent for writing," Cornelia said earnestly.

"Oh, dear, I wish my family were of your opinion. Mama treats my writing as if it were some manner of loathsome affliction and Papa says that it is high time I grew out of it and became more sensible."

"My aunt is of the same opinion. She is always telling me that I am in danger of being thought 'bookish.' "

"That is another accusation they hurl at me. Papa has even talked of locking me out of the library."

"Oh, it is a shame!" Cornelia cried. "You are most accomplished. I am sure that one day you will be published. I like your writing ever so much better than that of Selina Palgrave."

"Oh, do you?" Belinda breathed. "I think she is my favorite out of all the authors who write for Minerva Press. I do not see how you could compare me to *her*."

"I like your plots better too." Cornelia said.

"Not including *The Master of Melandre*! That was really frightening."

"Yes, even including the *Master*," Cornelia said. "Do continue."

"Very well." Belinda looked down at her manuscript. " 'As the carriage, drawn by six night-hued steeds, approached the top of the road, the shattered towers of Pendrake Hold' . . . 'shattered' or 'broken,' which do you prefer?"

"I think . . . 'broken' might be a little better," Cornelia said.

"So do I," Belinda agreed, searching for her place. "Umm . . . 'six night-hued' . . . no, 'broken' . . . 'broken towers rising over the tall elms that . . .' Oh, dear, I cannot continue. It is impossible for me to concentrate on this, when I keep remembering . . ." Belinda turned worried eyes on Cornelia. "I expect I should have not yielded to your persuasions. My book has not taken my mind off the c-coming meeting and it has not calmed my nerves. Why did you imagine that it would?"

Cornelia said quickly, "I hoped it might. And really, my dear, you ought not to anticipate the worst. You might find that you like him."

"I . . . I would not like him if he were Lord Byron himself, and you must admit that he is beautiful. I do not want to be married. I have been having such a good time. It . . . it is not fair to force me to this match. Did you know that there was a play written by Aphra Behn called *The Forc'd Marriage*? It was based on her own experience. She was forced into marriage against her will—"

"Who was Aphra Behn?" Cornelia asked.

"She was a playwright and a novelist and she lived in the seventeenth century and she was miserable, but fortunately, he died and she never married again."

"You would not want Lord Courtenay to—"

"No, of course I would not," Belinda interrupted. "I was talking about forced marriage. I do not think it is fair. Furthermore, supposing we do not suit."

"How could you not suit?" Cornelia demanded in some surprise. "He would have to look far and wide for a bride as beautiful and as intelligent as yourself, my dear. Many is the time that I have wished I looked like you."

"You?" Belinda stared at her in amazement. "Surely you are not serious! You are beautiful, Cornelia. I wish I had golden hair and blue eyes."

"My hair is blond, not golden, my dear, and half of the people in England are blue-eyed. Your hair is a lovely color and surely you ought to have had sandy lashes instead of your long dark lashes that curl at the ends, and I would have much preferred to have auburn hair. I might add that Beau Brummell and the dandies who sit in the bow window at White's did not declare me an Incomparable."

"I wish they had not bestowed that honor on me. It was no more than a week afterward that my family reminded me that I had been betrothed since birth and that I must marry Lord Courtenay . . . whom I do not even know."

"My dear," Cornelia said gently, "if he is not your slave by the time your meeting is at an end, he must possess a heart of stone."

"A heart of stone . . ." Belinda echoed. She rolled her eyes. "I might tell you, Cornelia, that the first time—the only time—we met, he threw a stone at me."

"Gracious, you will never tell me that!" Cornelia exclaimed.

"I do tell you that. It is true. I interrupted him while he was fishing and he lost the catch and his line as well. Of course, we were both much, much younger."

"How many years younger were you?" Cornelia inquired.

"Well . . ." Belinda blushed. "I had turned five and he was eleven."

"Oh, really, Belinda!" Cornelia exclaimed, caught between amusement and exasperation. "How can a meeting like that count for anything? You were both only children."

"I was terrified." Belinda grimaced. "He chased me afterward. I had to climb a tree and then I could not get down. I might have been there yet if Anthony had not ridden past. He was visiting my brother and he had come with us too." Belinda's eyes glowed. "Can you imagine, he climbed the tree and got me down."

"Anthony?" Cornelia repeated. "Who is Anthony?"

Belinda rolled her eyes. "I should not call him Anthony. Aunt Elizabeth heard me the other day and was quite exercised over it. I am speaking about Lord Furneaux."

"Lord Furneaux!" Cornelia exclaimed. "Oh, I have met him. I . . . do not know him very well, but I danced with him once at Almack's. He is a friend of your brother's?"

Belinda nodded. "Yes, they attended Eton and Oxford together and he used to come home with James. His parents died when he was twelve and his uncle was his guardian, but he was away quite a bit—so Anthony used to visit various friends from school. He was with us quite often. He and James are still very good friends and he also knows Aunt Elizabeth. She adores him."

"You never told me that!" Cornelia exclaimed.

"Did I not? I am surprised. I . . . I was deeply in love with him when I was little."

"You must have been very little when you knew him," Cornelia commented. "He is well into his thirties, so I am told."

"He is thirty-seven," Belinda corroborated with a sigh.

"Gracious, he's old enough to be your father."

"I have never thought of him as a father, I can assure you," Belinda said earnestly. "He was so kind to me. I cried and cried when he married Lady Anne Aubrey. He always used to say that he would wait for me to grow up."

Cornelia smiled and then sobered. "Poor man, his marriage did not last very long. She died in childbed, did she not?"

Belinda nodded. "Her child died with her. It would have been a girl. Fortunately, she had borne him a son. Jasper. He lives in the country. Oh, dear, I wish I might have been able to marry him."

"Is he anything like his father?" Cornelia asked interestedly.

"I would not know his father," Belinda said. "He died years ago."

"Oh," Cornelia said confusedly. "I was talking of Jasper."

"Jasper!" Belinda laughed. "He's only six. I meant Lord Furneaux. Do you know, I have the locket he gave me when I reached the age of ten. It is gold, and set with a tiny diamond. It is in my jewel box." She added ruefully, "Do you know, when he gave it to me, I had just read a book about a girl who had been given a golden locket by her own true love. I thought it was a love token . . . and the very same year, he married Lady Anne."

"Oh, dear, your heart must have been broken!"

"It was," Belinda said in acknowledgment.

"Well, I can understand that." Cornelia looked pensive. "He is certainly charming."

"He is lovely," Belinda agreed. "Oh, I wish he were not grieving for poor Lady Anne, but he is."

"So I have been told," Lady Cornelia said ruefully. She added, "But since you cannot marry Lord Furneaux, you had best put him out of your mind. Besides, you might find that you like Lord Courtenay now. After all, it is quite a few years since you last met."

"Well, I have no choice, have I? At least, I hope he is nothing like his brother, Edward. Oh, dear, I expect I should not speak ill of the dead, but I really did not like him and I have a feeling he was not drawn to me either. It was all arranged between our parents and now I have inherited his brother or he has inherited me. Our preferences are not to be consulted. It is all a matter of horrid bloodlines. I might as well be a brood mare for all the say I have in the matter." Belinda raised despairing eyes to Cornelia's face. "It would be delightful if, after all, he does not like me either. Please join me in praying that he does not."

"If your parents are so determined on the match, it would seem to me that it were better if he did like you," Cornelia said thoughtfully.

Belinda stamped her foot. "I do not want him to like me! Furthermore, I am determined not to like him, miniature or no miniature."

"Miniature? What miniature?" Cornelia asked.

Belinda regarded her with some surprise. "I did not tell you that his miniature was sent to me last week?"

"No, you did not."

"Well, it was, and if it is a good likeness, he is . . . very nice-looking. However, from all I have been able to ascertain, at least from such portraits as I have seen, Samuel Johnson was not nice-looking. He was scrofulous, in fact."

Cornelia regarded her with understandable amazement. "And what, pray, has Dr. Johnson's appearance to do with the likeness of your betrothed?"

"I am trying to make a point, Cornelia," Belinda said impatiently. "I am saying that as far as I am concerned, intelligence is more to be prized than a handsome appearance. If I had my choice, I would rather marry a poet or a novelist or a historian, and I should not care whether he was handsome or not."

"And what about Lord Furneaux, whose looks you have praised so extravagantly?" Cornelia demanded.

"I have explained that I would marry him above anyone else, but since there is no chance of that, I am merely saying that Lord Courtenay's good looks will not weigh with me. He is handsome, but he does not look as if he has ever opened a book, and furthermore, he became a soldier when he was very young. Consequently, I doubt that he had much time for reading. He will probably disapprove of my writing and . . ." She sighed. "Oh, dear, I know I will be perfectly miserable."

"I must tell you that you could as easily be perfectly miserable were you married to a man of letters. My brother was at Eton with Bysshe Shelley and said he was a 'damned loose screw.' "

"Men of letters are not all cut from the same cloth," Belinda said loftily. "But that is aside from the point. I do not mind telling you, Cornelia, that I think we should be allowed to choose whom and whom not we wish to marry."

"But, my dear," Cornelia said reasonably, "that is not the way it is done, unless there is one of those horrid Gretna Green elopements."

"Horrid?" Belinda's eyes suddenly gleamed with mischief. "I think it would be ever so exciting to run away with a man you love."

"The thing is that *he* does not always wed *her*," Cornelia said sagely. "And then, of course, she is disgraced for life and must needs live in seclusion, generally in some obscure country town where no one knows her. That is what happened to Sarah Treadwell, whom we both knew in school, if you will remember."

Belinda pulled a face. "I do remember her

very well. It is my feeling that her possible bridegroom got to know Sarah better on the way to Scotland and that is why they did not marry."

Cornelia's rather austere manner disintegrated into giggles. "Indeed, I am sure you are right. I could not bear Sarah's company for an hour, much less the length of time it must take to reach the Scottish border."

Belinda laughed and then sobered. "I wonder what he will think of me?"

"Well, you are meeting him a month before your wedding day. My sister Julia, as you know, met her bridegroom three days before they were to wed."

"Oh, dear, I do remember. Poor Julia wept all the way to the altar."

"I assure you that she laughs about that now. She is very happy with him. I am soon to be an aunt."

Belinda nodded. "That is the reason I am being forced to marry Lord Courtenay. The present earl, his father, had only the two sons, and his wife cannot have any more children. Lord Gerald is the last of the line and consequently they want more than one heir. I am to marry him and provide that heir. My preferences do not matter, and nor, I suspect, do his."

"My dear." Cornelia put a comforting arm around her friend's waist. "If you find him too disagreeable, I am sure you will not be forced to marry him. I cannot believe that they would insist."

"If they do not insist," Belinda said in a

hard little voice, "I will be sent home for the sin of having been declared an Incomparable. And I expect that my parents were not too pleased about the ball at the Italian opera house. However, I am sure that they will make us marry. Papa and Gerald's father Lord Beresford are the best of friends and Aunt Elizabeth is adamant on the subject and everybody listens to her."

"Your ladyship," said a concerned voice from the doorway. "You must get dressed."

Belinda turned toward the owner of the voice, her abigail, Mary, whose big blue eyes were filled with distress. "I will be there presently."

"But, milady," the girl protested, "his lordship will be here at any moment."

"I know when he is coming, Mary. I will be with you directly."

Mary, appearing even more concerned, went reluctantly out of the room as Belinda turned to Cornelia. "It will be horrid if we loathe each other on sight."

"You *have* praised the miniature," Cornelia reminded her. "And I do not see how he could possibly loathe *you*. But had you not better go to Mary?"

"I will, of course, poor girl. If I am late, she will be called to account. But, oh, Cornelia, I do so dislike this situation! It is so entirely demeaning to be passed from one brother to the other like a . . . a sack of oats."

"My dearest, were he to look upon you as a sack of oats, he would be in no condition to marry you, for surely he would be soft in the head and better confined to Bedlam!" Cornelia giggled.

Belinda also giggled. "You do cheer me, Cornelia," she said gratefully and fondly as she hurried out of the chamber.

Lord Gerald Courtenay, surveying himself in the long glass that stood in his dressing room, said, "It looks very well, Robert, even though I am not sure that it is me."

His valet, being used to his master's sense of humor, smiled. "I think you will have no difficulty becoming used to these garments, sir."

"I will take your word for that." Lord Courtenay's gaze traveled dubiously over the tight-fitting double-breasted claret-hued coat, the tight gray unmentionables, and the gold-tasseled black boots, champagne-polished to a high shine. He was used to seeing himself in the scarlet-and-gold uniform of a captain in the Fifteenth Light Dragoons. He did not mind his new guise, but he found his high starched neckcloth uncomfortable. Not only did it scratch his chin, but it kept it at an awkward angle. When he had more time, he would have to remonstrate with Robert regarding that neckcloth. He cherished no ambition to out-Brummell the Beau.

He sighed, regretting the loss of his uniform or, more specifically, his command. He regretted even more the reasons for the pair of visits which must take up the better part of this particular afternoon. Both promised to be difficult and both held a strong quotient of anguish.

The first, however, was by far the worse or, he frowned, was it the second, upon which the first was predicated? He groaned and gazed upward, recognizing weather that reflected his mood. Gray-tipped clouds floated over the sun, alternately darkening and lightening the earth beneath. Felice would describe the effect as *chiaroscuro*. Felice.

He groaned, envisioning her lovely face and exquisite little body. He had seen her all too seldom in the year that had passed since their first meeting.

In his mind's eye was that never-to-be-forgotten moment when on searching for the lodgings of one Angela Sciarroni, a dancer with the Italian opera, he had knocked at the wrong door and, a second later, gazed with wonder at the gloriously beautiful face of Mlle. Felice D'Aubigny. The effect had not been marred in the least by the green smears of paint on one cheek. There had been more paint on her smock, her fingers, and on the brush she held in one small graceful hand. In the midst of his stuttered apologies, he had become mesmerized by her beauty and her charm. It had been, as she later confessed to him, an enchanted moment for her as well.

A second groan escaped him as he thought of the miniature he had sent to the Lady Belinda Devereux. It was one of a pair painted by Felice and originally intended for his mother and his aunt. He had kept them both. He had preferred to keep Felice's work for himself. He had little dreamed that within the year, one of those delicate paintings would have to be given to the girl once destined to be his brother's bride and now . . . Tears blurred his vision.

In a regrettably short time he would have a woeful confidence for his beautiful and adored little mistress. He would be forced to tell her that due to the nesting grouse which had risen up in front of his elder brother, Edward, causing his horse to rear just as he was recklessly using both hands to aim at a bird in flight, he, Gerald, had become the heir to an earldom.

The accident had left him racked by two separate griefs. One was, of course, for the early demise of his poor brother. The other and far more poignant grief was for the pending loss of his mistress. Again he cused the fate that had caused Edward to be thrown from his horse, landing on the rock that had shattered his skull. That same rock had shattered his own life too. Now he had to marry that homely carrot-topped chit, whom he had met but once in his life!

Despite her far-from-prepossessing appearance, she was not only very rich, but she could trace her lineage back to one Sieur Devereux, who had ridden into England in the train of William the Conqueror—and would that the ship bearing him across the turbulent channel had sunk!

He imagined that Felice would understand. The French, too, were compelled to marry without love and for the sake of the dowry and the family. Had poor Felice had not been thrust from her native Normandy, escaping her country hidden under a load of cabbages, she, too, would have been married to the Comte . . . whoever, who had perished on the guillotine at the age of sixteen. Though, to be absolutely honest, Gerald could not actually mourn the death of that hapless aristocrat. Felice's own tragic tale had ridden with Gerald into many a battle against her countrymen. Several had died at the point of his sword and several others had been dispatched by a well-aimed bullet, all rushed into the next world with his muttered, *"Pour la belle Felice!"*

He grimaced. The nearer he came to her dwelling, the more reluctant he was to tell her about his pending nuptials. Unfortunately, the die had been cast, the day named, and this afternoon he would offer for the little wretch—a mere formality, of course.

He had received that particular intelligence this morning, since, because of prior commitments, he had been unable to spend the previous night with Felice. He flushed. The commitments in question had entailed a session at White's with some old cronies. They had paired off for piquet, and he, beginning with a losing streak, had ended the night some five hundred pounds richer.

He would not tell her that, of course. He would give her the excuse of a regimental dinner. Unfortunately, he would have to cut this visit short as well. He had to present himself at the home of his bride-to-be or, rather, at the home of her formidable Great-Aunt Elizabeth Guest, Countess of Waltham.

It was Lady Elizabeth whom he suspected of being one of the prime movers in these hasty nuptials.

Evidently little Belinda had not been behaving herself or, rather, she had not met Lady Elizabeth's exacting standards of what she considered Proper Behavior for Peeresses. Despite her unappealing appearance, the chit seemed to possess a liveliness of disposition which had led her into some questionable situations. His father had mentioned a ball at the Italian opera house and a race through the park with Lord Alvanley, which she had evidently won. Who had taken her to the opera house? he wondered. Probably her escort had been some fortune hunter. He could not imagine that anyone could have been attracted to anything save her fortune—as for Alvanley, he would have found her amusing, no doubt. Yet, she was rather a nice little thing.

On the one occasion they had met, she had danced up to him just as he had been about to land a fine trout, one that had eluded him all that summer. Her unexpected arrival had caused him to drop the rod, losing the fish. He had hurled a stone at her, fortunately missing her.

However, the deed had been witnessed by his brother, who had promptly told on him, something Belinda had not done. He had been severely chastised by his tutor. He groaned. In a regrettably short time he would be offering for that same little wretch with the flaming hair that framed a freckled countenance only a mother could love! He, Gerald Courtenay, forced to resign from his regiment, something he had hated to do, was now knuckling under to family pressure in the name of his late brother, this despite the fact that he loved Felice D'Aubigny with all his heart and would continue to love her until he died. Another groan escaped him as he found himself in front of the house containing her studio or, as he was fond of calling it, Paradise.

A few minutes later he was tapping lightly on the door of her studio, wondering belatedly if she were there. Then, before his fears had a chance to crystallize, he heard her voice. "Who is there, please?"

" 'Tis I, Gerald," he called.

"Ah, Gerald!" She pulled open the door and smiled up at him, looking even more beautiful than he remembered. The coloring of his bride-to-be and her appearance would be as Caliban to Helen of Troy, he decided as he gazed into huge blue eyes fringed with improbably long dark lashes, a contrast to her wheat-gold hair. Her nose was perfect and her mouth invited kisses. She was not tall. Her head reached his heart, he thought, the heart she possessed. Her shape was exquisite. It seemed made for the high-waisted muslins with their vaguely Grecian outlines so popular in these years. However, on this occasion she was wearing a paint-spattered smock, and with a pang he saw that as she had when first he met her, she was holding a tiny paintbrush in one delicate little hand.

"You are at work, then?" he asked disappointedly.

"Ah, that is a strange greeting." She gave him a provocative glance. "You do not say even, *'Bonjour, Felice'*?"

"Of course I say, *'Bonjour, Felice'*!" Moving inside, he took her in his arms and pressed a long kiss on her lips, which she rapturously returned.

Moving back from him finally, she said, "I will correct you, *mon amour*. I *was* at work, but I will now put away my brushes even though you have been *très méchant*. I know that you returned yesterday from seeing your parents . . . yet, you did not return to me and I waited for you all the long, long night."

There were equal amounts of shame and pleasure mirrored in his eyes as he kissed her yet again. "It was not possible, my love," he sighed. "You see—"

She held up her hand, silencing the excuses that were trembling on his lips. "You need not give me an explanation. It is enough that you are here. And now that you have left the army, we will have time and time and time together. But . . ." Her eyes were suddenly filled with anxiety. "What is it, Gerald? All is not well with you, my dearest. I read it in your gaze."

He had meant to break the news gently that was causing lumps in his throat and a tightness in his chest, but much to his subsequent chagrin, it burst forth from him like a storm-sent wave battering down a seawall. "I am to be married in a month's time, Felice."

Her slender body tensed. She stared up at him incredulously. *"Non!"* she whispered.

"*Non!*" Her voice became louder. "You . . . you do not tell me this! *Non, non, non, c'est impossible!* It is the joke, *oui*? You are funning me, *n'est-ce pas*?" She fixed her eyes on his face. "But I . . . I think it is true what you have just told me, yes?"

"Yes," he said bitterly, "it is true. Yet, I can call it a joke too, a cruel joke played upon us by fate. This marriage is none of my desiring. I am to wed my brother's bride."

"You . . . you will marry his widow?" she demanded confusedly.

He shook his head. "She is not his widow. She is the Lady Belinda Devereux, the daughter of the Earl of Carlow. She was betrothed to my brother. I have met her but once in my life."

"And, as it was with Dante and his Beatrice, you fell in love with her at first sight?" she demanded in a hard little voice.

A mirthless laugh escaped him. "On the contrary, my dear, she was five and I was eleven. We had an altercation and I was whipped and sent to bed without my supper."

"But . . . but it is barbaric!" she cried. "Why should you take to your heart the bride of your late brother?"

He grimaced. "Be assured, my dearest, that I have not and I never will take the bride of my late brother to my heart. It is a family matter. Surely you, a Frenchwoman, must understand about bloodlines?"

"I . . . ah, yes, I do understand." Felice looked down and shook her head. She said sadly, "My Aunt Jeanne often laments that I, a D'Aubigny, lost the Comte de . . . But no matter, we will not talk about that. *Ah, la vie est cruelle, c'est vrai.*"

"Yes," he agreed bitterly. "And never crueler than now. If my poor brother had not died, all would be different."

"*La mort*," she groaned. "If my kindred had not perished beneath the blade of the guillotine, I, a D'Aubigny, would not have lain with you like some whore from the Parisian bordellos. And that is how you must regard me—as your whore."

"Oh, my dearest, my love, my only love," he cried brokenly. "I cannot bear to hear you describe yourself in such ugly terms! You know how much I love you! My dearest, to me you are an angel from heaven. You are everything that is good and beautiful. This damned marriage was none of my planning."

She gave him a reproachful look. "You, a hero of the wars, can allow yourself to be so easily manipulated by your family?"

"You do not understand," he began unhappily, wishing that the one explanation he could offer were not something that would deal a bitter blow to her pride. Yet, he thought uncomfortably, it was highly unlikely in France, where the dowry, or *dot*, was even more highly prized, that a young man married his mistress, even if he loved her to distraction. Truthfully, he did not see how he could love Felice any more fervently than he did already. She possessed his heart and his soul, but in France, too, people married for the sake of family and future generations, and, he guessed, they were no happier than he would be.

Actually, he thought ruefully, were Felice to agree, there was no reason why they need renounce their love. His father had never let his marital obligations interfere with his passion for one Ruth Campion of Drury Lane. Before Mrs. Campion, there had been an opera dancer and, he thought with a sudden surge of hope, why could he not follow in his father's footsteps? There was no reason why he could not continue to see Felice.

"What do I not understand?" Felice asked.

He started. He had been so concentrated on the plan that was currently taking shape in his mind that he had actually forgotten where he was. "I beg your pardon, my love." He kissed her. "You *are* my love, you know."

"And you are mine," she cried passionately. "But," she sighed, "do not imagine that I am unaware of your situation. I understand these family obligations and I beg you to pardon me for taxing you with my megrims. It is only that . . . that I cannot bear the thought of losing you."

"You will not lose me, *mon ange*." Gerald kissed her again. "I must marry, I must beget an heir, but I could no more stop seeing you than I could cut out my heart. You *are* my heart, my love."

"And you know what you mean to me," she whispered, pressing herself against him.

"Felice, my devine Felice!" Lifting her and holding her against his chest, he deposited her on the long soft couch where her customers sat for the preliminary sketches she made before commencing a miniature. Between loving little kisses, he began to outline his plans to her.

"Lord Furneaux!" Belinda cried excitedly. "He is here . . . now?" She stamped her foot. "Why did you not tell me immediately, Mary?"

"I had to dress you, milady," her abigail said composedly. "I could not have you wriggling about when I had all these pesky buttons to slip into these tiny little slits. I would like to have a word with the mantua-maker, I would. It is high time she thought of us who has to do for you."

"Oh, bother the mantua-maker, Mary! When did he arrive? Oh, I have been thinking about him all the day. And," she added belatedly, "I would not have wriggled about. I am a young lady now and . . . Oh, dear, I simply must see him. I am all done, am I not?" Without waiting for her abigail's response, Belinda rushed out of the room. Then, tardily reminding herself that she was a young lady, three months into her eighteenth year, she walked decorously down the stairs. As she made her descent, she prayed that his lordship had not yet taken his leave. It would be terrible were she not to see him, this man who had been occupying her thoughts for the past hour and with whom she would be in love for the rest of her life, bridegroom or no bridegroom! If only her love might be requited, but it never would be.

Even without the years that stretched between them, and the complication of her coming betrothal, she could never, as she had said to Cornelia, compete with the beautiful young wife who had died so tragically. He had mourned his lost lady ever since her early demise, and according to her brother James, Lord Furneaux was the very prototype of the constant lover.

Her unhappy reflections had carried her across the hall and into the drawing room, where her Aunt Elizabeth was deep in conversation with her unexpected guest. As she moved away from the threshold, Belinda remembered belatedly that she ought to have knocked or, rather, that she probably ought not to have come in at all. She read annoyance in Lady Elizabeth's stare, but there was nothing but pleasure reflected in Lord Furneaux's eyes as he rose to greet her.

"My dearest Belinda," he said warmly. "What is this I have been hearing about you?" Moving toward her, he caught her hand and carried it to his lips, saying as he released it, "I think you are even more beautiful than you were the last time we met."

"I do thank you, my lord." Belinda curtsied, wishing at the same time that she might return his compliment. She had forgotten how incredibly handsome he was! The white streak in his black hair, present since the untimely death of his wife, only served to accentuate the surrounding darkness of his waving locks. His eyes, a golden hazel, were shaded by incredibly long lashes, and to her mind, his features resembled a bust of Apollo she had seen in the British Museum. For the rest, his shoulders were broad and his waist narrow. He was easily eleven inches over five feet, and as usual, he ignored fashion by being casually dressed in garments more comfortable than stylish. Yet, at the same time, they suited him so admirably that he appeared quite as well-turned-out as Beau Brummell.

"And so," he said genially, "I am told you are on the very brink of betrothal, my dear."

Scanning his face for the look of disappointment she hoped to find, Belinda could discover none. She produced a brave smile. "Yes, my lord, it is true. He will be here later this afternoon."

"Within the hour," Lady Elizabeth amplified, her cold blue gaze on Belinda's face. "As I was telling you, Anthony, I think they should dwell together very well. The young man has been with Wellington's forces on the Peninsula and I gather that he has not formed any previous attachments. That is, I believe, most fortunate."

"I am in complete agreement, Lady Elizabeth." Lord Furneaux turned toward Belinda. "The Courtenays, my dear, are an old family, a distinguished clan of which one might say 'all the brothers were valiant and all the sisters virtuous.'"

"Oh, from the tomb of the Duchess of Newcastle!" Belinda exclaimed. "I do love that quotation. The duchess was an author too."

"Too? *Too*, is it?" Lady Elizabeth bent a stern glance on her great-niece. "To whom does 'too' refer? Not to yourself, I hope. It is high time that you ceased your scribbling, my girl."

"I cannot agree, Lady Elizabeth," Lord Furneaux said quickly. "Belinda used to compose charming verses, even when she was little. To my mind, she has a real feeling for poetic imagery."

"You . . . you remember my poems?" Belinda regarded him in delighted surprise.

"Indeed I do," he assured her. "And are you still composing poetry or have you tried your hand at a novel, as I think I once suggested?"

"You did, my lord, and I followed that suggestion. I have written two novels," she said shyly.

"You will have to let me read them. And . . ." He paused as Lady Cornelia appeared in the doorway. She looked surprised and pleased as she saw the visitor.

"Lord Furneaux!" she exclaimed.

"Lady Cornelia." He came to bow over her hand. "I did not know you were in town."

"I arrived last week," she said.

"And how is your aunt?"

"Her health is improving. She is staying with my cousin in Bath."

"Ah, taking the waters, I presume?"

"Ugh, the waters!" Belinda interjected, making a little face. "I hate the taste of them."

"So does my aunt," Cornelia said. "However, she has always found the city enchanting."

Lord Furneaux laughed. "Usually it is the other way around."

"I think it is a charming city," Belinda said.

"I am particularly interested in the Roman ruins."

"As am I," Lord Furneaux observed. "The traces of Roman culture in Britain are always fascinating."

"And you find them in so many unexpected places," Cornelia said. "Sometimes I would like to follow the legions, as it were. I think I would start in the north with the wall."

"That is an idea that appeals to me too," Lord Furneaux began, but whatever else he might have said was interrupted by the butler's appearance and his announcement that Lord Courtenay had arrived.

"Oh, dear, I think I must return to the library," Cornelia said quickly. She added shyly, "It was a pleasure seeing you again, my lord."

"It was my pleasure entirely, Lady Cornelia," he said warmly.

"Ah," Lady Elizabeth said as Cornelia curtsied and withdrew, "I am glad your suitor has arrived." She bent a stern look on Belinda. "Come and sit here, child"—she indicated a straight-backed chair, its arms ending in swan's wings—"ridiculous thing that it is . . . though I must say that swan's wings are preferable to crocodile heads and sphinx busts."

Lord Furneaux's golden eyes gleamed with amusement. "I must agree." He nodded. "Lord Nelson's victories have had a most deleterious effect on furniture design." He bowed as he said to Lady Elizabeth, "It has been delightful to see you again and"—he turned to Belinda—"you, my dear. I do wish you happy."

"I thank you, my lord," Belinda said in a small voice, wishing with all her heart that it was Lord Courtenay who was leaving and Lord Furneaux arriving to ask for her hand in marriage.

After Lady Elizabeth had exchanged farewells with Lord Furneaux, she took advantage of the brief moment before Lord Courtenay was shown into the drawing room to hiss, "Sit up straight. You are drooping like a wilted peony."

Belinda sighed and straightened up. "There," she murmured with another, longer sigh.

"Do not sigh!" Lady Elizabeth frowned. "You are not being tossed onto an ash heap or being sold into slavery. You are . . ." She paused as the butler announced importantly, "Lord Courtenay."

Belinda, glaring up at his unwelcome lordship, received a distinct shock. Though, as she realized very quickly, it was utterly stupid of her, she had actually been expecting a larger version of that horrid boy who had once heaved a good-size stone at her. Consequently, it was with considerable difficulty that she managed to keep her mouth from falling open as she saw the tall, darkly handsome young man advancing into the drawing room. Her first thought was that the butler had made some mistake. This fashionably dressed gentleman could not be that gangly lad who had glared at her out of narrowed brown eyes and who had called her all sorts of rude names in addition to heaving the stone at her. He had almost hit her, too, she remembered, and then banished the episode from her thoughts. In so doing, she, who had not taken her eyes from his face, realized that he was staring at her in a puzzled way, as if he, also, could not believe what he was seeing. It was time and past that she corrected that impression, she thought ruefully, for she ought to have curtsied, which she did, saying softly, "Good afternoon, Lord Courtenay. It is p-pleasant to . . . to see you again."

"Yes, for me also, Lady Belinda." He reddened. "You *are* Lady Belinda, are you not?"

"Of course she is," Lady Elizabeth said. She continued, "I was not aware that you knew each other."

"We do not," Belinda said quickly. "We met once, but it was a long time ago."

"A very long time ago," Lord Courtenay agreed. "Indeed, it has been at least . . ."

"Thirteen years," Belinda interpolated. "I was five."

"I was eleven." He nodded, thinking that the girl before him could not possibly have been that scrawny freckle-faced carrot-top who had caused him to lose his fish.

"Well," Lady Elizabeth said with her characteristic bluntness, "does she please you?"

"Aunt Elizabeth," Belinda groaned, feeling her face grow hot.

Gerald, shocked by her ladyship's bald question, found himself in a quandary. It seemed to him that Felice D'Aubigny, sole possessor of his mind's eyes, was backing off, startled as he was startled by the radiant little beauty before him. Still, since his common sense told him that it was impossible to have been captivated so quickly, he did not utter the several encomiums that rose to his lips. He said simply and not in answer to Lady Elizabeth's outrageous question, "I am delighted to meet you again after all these years, Lady Belinda."

"I have been looking forward to seeing you again." Belinda smiled.

"As have I," he said, thinking that her smile was devastating, but somehow Felice had slipped back into his consciousness, and mentally he welcomed her with an analogy which pleased him.

His beautiful mistress was like a brilliantly polished diamond, while the girl before him was also a diamond, but one which had not yet received the jeweler's needful attentions. At this moment in time, he preferred polish. Yet, despite that preference, should he not say something flattering to little Lady Belinda? That, he told himself rather bitterly, was not necessary. He had not come to pay court to her. He had come to offer for her, and at least he was more willing to fulfill that obligation than he had been earlier in the day or, rather, the week.

"Lord Courtenay," Lady Elizabeth said in a voice that was like a slash across the wrist, "I assume that Belinda does please you?"

Mentally he decried her bluntness, but at least it would serve to bring matters to a close. He nodded. "Yes, of course she does."

The smile that accompanied his words was hard to achieve this time, mainly because he was beginning to feel very sorry for the girl. It was possible that she, too, had preferences that did not include himself, but, again, those preferences were not accompanied by freedom of choice. Still, something more had to be said. "Do I please you, my dear?" he asked.

"Of course you please her, Gerald," Lady Elizabeth said impatiently. "She would certainly be a great ninny if you did not!"

Gerald, glancing at Belinda, saw that the poor child had tensed, as well she might, he thought compassionately, and angrily too. All animation had fled from her lovely face and she was avoiding his gaze now. He opened his mouth and closed it as Lady Elizabeth continued, "Very good. All is right and tight, then. The banns will be read in the Church of St. James's on the next three Sundays. I will expect you to escort your fiancée to church on Sunday next." She turned to Belinda. "I am of the opinion that you will deal extremely well together. I myself was wed by decree rather than desire and I can tell you that there has not been a day that I have not missed my dear husband. We had forty years of happiness and I a convinced that you will be very happy too. And—"

"Lady Elizabeth," Gerald interrupted.

"Well, my lord?" she demanded crisply.

"Please, there is something I would like to say to Lady Belinda."

She looked surprised and not entirely pleased. She said gruffly, "Well, say it, then."

Belinda looked up at him, feeling . . . But she was not sure what she was feeling, save that she wished Lady Elizabeth would leave the room and allow them a moment alone. It was not right that she should remain there, presiding over them as though they were a pair of convicted criminals and she their warden.

Gerald moved closer to Belinda. He said solemnly, "Lady Belinda, will you do me the honor of giving me your hand in marriage?"

"But that has all been decided, my dear boy," Lady Elizabeth snapped.

"I beg your pardon, Lady Elizabeth," Gerald said coolly, "but I think I must be allowed to propose to Lady Belinda. A proposal is customary before a marriage, is it not?"

Lady Elizabeth appeared slightly taken aback, but she said, "I must beg your pardon, my lad. You are quite right." She turned to Belinda. "You have heard the question, my dear. What is your answer?"

Gerald said shortly, "I believe that it is I who must ask that question. Will you marry me, Lady Belinda?"

Belinda blinked and, much to her surprise, felt tears in her eyes. Before he had entered the room, she had expected . . . But now was not the time to dwell on those expectations. She said with a tremulous smile, "I will marry you, my lord."

"I thank you, my dear," he said gravely. "I will do my utmost to make you happy." He caught her hand and bore it to his lips.

*   *   *

Some twenty minutes later, Cornelia, once more ensconced in the library, was just sealing a letter when the door was thrust open and Belinda hurried in, looking bemused and tearful. Cornelia rose swiftly, "Oh, my dear, what is amiss?"

"N-nothing. He . . . he . . ." Belinda put a hand to her eyes and swallowed convulsively.

"My dear, did he not offer for you?"

"He did offer for me, Cornelia, even though Aunt Elizabeth assured him that it was not necessary as long as I pleased *him*. I expect she was only trying to flatter him, because, naturally, it has all been decided. She said that flat out."

"Oh, my dear, she did not!" Cornelia exclaimed indignantly.

"She did . . . and I could see he was annoyed. He insisted on offering for me and obtaining *my* consent."

"You did not give it?" her mystified friend asked.

"I did. I had no choice, you know that. And, Cornelia, he is very handsome and kind. He says he will . . . will do his best to make me happy." More tears trickled down Belinda's face.

"But why, might I ask, are you weeping, then?" Cornelia demanded.

"B-because he is so kind and I . . . I ought to like him. I do *like* him, but . . . but I still love Lord Furneaux, and he . . . he never even looks at me, not in any *interesting* way, I mean."

"Oh, my dearest," Cornelia said after a slight

pause. "You cannot love Lord Furneaux—as you yourself said, he is still grieving over his late wife."

"I . . . I wish that I were an opera dancer!" Belinda sobbed.

"An . . . an opera dancer?" Cornelia regarded her with total confusion. "What, pray, has an opera dancer to do with anything?"

"He appears to like them," Belinda sighed.

"Oh, my dear, I can only think that that is mere gossip!" Cornelia exclaimed.

"No, it is not, really. I expect I ought not to talk about it, but I know for a fact that he has kept more than one. Sir Colin Wooldrige, who was courting me at the beginning of the Season, told me so."

"I do not believe you should know about these things." Cornelia frowned.

"I daresay I should not, but I do, and you do too. And, of course, she—whoever the chit is—cannot take the place of his late wife. Oh, Cornelia, did you not think him beautiful?"

"Lord Furneaux is very well-looking," Cornelia said rather repressively. "Tell me about Lord Courtenay, my dear."

"What is there to tell?" Belinda shrugged. "We will be married in a month. He *was* much more pleasant than I had anticipated. He is just as dark as Lord Furneaux and he has brown eyes. I knew that, but they seem larger than they did all those years ago . . . of course, they would be. He is very handsome."

"Well, I am certainly glad that you approve him, Belinda," Cornelia said.

"I did not say that I approved him. I was

just surprised to see how very much he has changed, that is all. And I did appreciate the fact that he insisted on offering for me even though I am quite sure that he is no more enthusiastic about the match than I. It is just that he must have an heir." With a little gulping sob, Belinda added, "Oh, Cornelia, there ought to be more to marriage than that, do you not agree?"

"Of course I agree, my dear. And judging from all you have said, I cannot believe that you will be as unhappy as you seem to fear."

"Do you not?" Belinda, meeting Cornelia's sympathetic gaze, wondered if she believed in those assurances. She had a definite feeling that, as usual, Cornelia was trying to comfort her. It was on the tip of her tongue to ask her . . . But what difference would it have made? No matter what her friend believed or did not believe, she was committed to this marriage, and only a major cataclysm could prevent it. Since neither earthquake nor typhoon nor tempest had troubled the city of London in recent years, it was rather futile to hope that one or another would arise on her wedding day.

2

Gerald was dreaming. In his dream, he was watching a mammoth force of cavalry, mounted on huge steeds. The flanks of their mounts were heaving, their eyes rolled wildly, and their snorting was almost as loud as the cries of their riders as, rushing over the parched yellow roads leading into some nameless Spanish town, they surrounded his embattled corps. Though they fought bravely, his men were hopelessly outnumbered, and one after another they fell before the terrible onslaught. And who was it mounted on the immense black horse, the horse with the flaming eyes, a giant creature risen from hell, that always troubled his sleep before a battle? He could not see the face of that rider but, as always, that presence filled him with a sense of impending doom.

"Gerald, love, wake up, wake up, please," a soft voice urged.

Gerald opened his eyes immediately, blinking against the sunlight. Then, meeting the vibrant gaze of Felice, he stared back at her

40

in melancholy appreciation. She stood near the bed, her fair curls tousled, but otherwise she was neatly garbed in her paint-bedaubed smock over a white muslin gown.

The black horse, harbinger of trouble, faded from his mind as he looked up at her beautiful face. Then it was back, galloping through his head as it had pounded across the parched landscape of his dream. He groaned and banished a vision which certainly should not have troubled him on this, his wedding morning.

He exhaled a long sigh as his eyes wandered over Felice's slender body and he remembered her lying in his arms throughout the night. She had been loving and giving then, but at present her gaze was cool. The ecstasy they had shared in the long reaches of the night might never have taken place. That was evident in the way she had woken him. There had been no kisses, no tantalizing little touches, only her voice, soft and, he realized now, cold.

"Oh, God, Felice," he sighed, stretching his hand and letting it fall to the bed as she stepped back out of reach.

"You must get dressed and go home, Gerald," she said.

"Damn, I do not want to leave you," he protested.

"You have said that you have no choice," she reminded him.

"I have not, I beg you to believe me," he said earnestly. "I could be a puppet pulled by strings. It was the same with my father, and probably my grandfather as well. The name.

The blood. The traditions. Those are my strings, Felice, and what I would not give to sever them. I would have severed them, had it not been for my poor brother—"

She held up a quelling hand. "We have spoken of these things before, Gerald. There is no need to go over them again. We are not the first to have been undone by fate. With you, it was your brother's hunting accident. With me, it was my country's revolution. But enough! You must leave, my love."

"Yes," he agreed reluctantly. "And, of course, you know that save for that portion required to keep me alive, you have the greater part of my heart, my darling."

"And you have mine." She suddenly relented and moved to the bed. She did not protest as he ruthlessly pulled her down beside him, embracing her passionately.

At thirty minutes past the hour of ten, Belinda, wearing a lacy white gown, stared discontentedly into the mirror attached to her armoire. She turned to Cornelia, who was also in white and, to Belinda's mind, looking very lovely in a hue that perfectly suited her golden beauty. She said, "I wish I might have been married in green, the green of new spring leaves."

Cornelia did not seem surprised by this comment, mainly because she had heard it off and on each time she had accompanied Belinda to a fitting in the upstairs sewing room. "Green is quite your best color," she agreed. "It does bring out your eyes, but you heard Mrs. Oliver." Imitating that lady's lofty manner and affected speech, she said, "In this year of 1813, it is *de rigueur* for all brides to wear white . . . white for purity and for an unblemished character."

"I happen to believe that one can appear unblemished in green as well as white. My great-grandmother wore blue and my mother's wedding gown was rose-colored. Neither lady was brought to bed of an early child."

"Belinda!" Cornelia exclaimed. "You shock me!"

"You mean that you ought to have been shocked, but you are not." Belinda giggled.

Cornelia also laughed. "Well, perhaps, but white is a hue that is very becoming to you, my dear. And the gown is beautiful. Mrs. Oliver has exceeded herself."

"I beg you will not speak to me about Mrs. Oliver," Belinda flared. "I do dislike the woman." Belinda pulled a face. "She is so toplofty, acting as if she were doing me a favor by making my gown—when *she* did not really make it. Each time I came into the sewing room, I found her poor little slavey, Jane, hard at work on it. I am sure that she had a hand in its designing as well."

"I am sure she did," Cornelia agreed. "She is clever with her needle. I had half a mind to challenge that woman on her behalf myself."

"I am glad you did not. Aunt Elizabeth would have been furious and"—Belinda smiled mischievously—"Mrs. Oliver does have a nose for news, you cannot deny that."

"No, I cannot," Cornelia affirmed. "I would

never have heard about Madame de Staël's
'horrid' way of putting herself forward, and
nor would I have heard the latest tidbit about
Lord Byron and Caroline Lamb. Though I
was certainly shocked at Mrs. Oliver's laughing at the way he walks. It is no joke to have
a crippled foot and be forced to go on tiptoe."

"I agree." Belinda frowned. "I can tell you
that I would not mind suiting my steps to
his."

"Belinda!" Cornelia exclaimed. "What are
you saying?"

"I am saying that I wish I knew Lord Byron
and I am sure you wish the same thing, even
though Lord Furneaux says that he is very
moody and, on occasion, can be extremely
sharp-tongued."

"I imagine that his infirmity is very wearing and—" Cornelia broke off as the clock on
the mantelshelf chimed the quarter-hour. "My
dear, what can be the matter with us, sitting
here chattering and the wedding due to take
place in little more than an hour! We must be
at the church."

"The church is no very great distance from
here," Belinda said over a sudden pounding
in her throat. "But I expect we must soon go
down. The other bridesmaids will be there at
eleven and Papa will soon be arriving to escort me." She frowned. "I expected that he
might come and see me last night, but as you
know, he did not."

"Probably he arrived late," Cornelia said.

"Did I not tell you that he arrived at six
o'clock?" Belinda asked.

"No, you did not." Cornelia shook her head.

"Well, I was in a great pother last night, to be sure, but he did arrive at six o'clock and sent word that he was wearied from the exigencies of travel. I have never been his favorite, you know."

"Oh, I am sure he can have no favorites among you," Cornelia said quickly.

"He has," Belinda said positively. "He loves Kate the most. She *is* very beautiful and, of course, she is the firstborn. I think he loves her even more than he does Peter."

"More than his eldest son? I can hardly believe that!" Cornelia exclaimed.

"I assure you that he does. He has already let her do exactly as she pleases. Fancy, she fell in love with Sir Athol Strathendon, even while Papa was in negotiations for her to marry Lord Cheyne, but she would not have it. She had a terrible argument with Papa, but ultimately she prevailed, something none of the rest of us have ever been able to do. I wrote at least five letters to Papa begging him not to force me to this match, but he wrote back and said that it was all settled and that he did not care for my attitude. My sister Meg could tell you a similar story, and so could Peter and James. I expect it will be no different when Pansy comes of age. He does as he chooses with our lives."

"My dear," Cornelia sighed, "that is the way fathers are. If Mama had not been widowed so early, I am sure that my brother would not have been allowed to marry Ellen Cunningham, who barely had a feather to fly with.

Mama was much exercised over it, but he talked her round."

"And she used part of what would have been your dowry to help them. That was not fair!" Belinda said roundly.

"It was well she did—with the children coming so quickly," Cornelia said. "And after all, there is my aunt for whom I am partially named. She insists on settling something on me."

"And so she should. You have certainly been good to her, staying with her and tending her when you could have been invited to a score of places where you could really have enjoyed yourself. You are too good, Cornelia. I will miss you. I am so glad that Aunt Elizabeth wants you to stay on. She has taken one of her fancies to you, which means we will be able to see each other once I am back in London again. Oh, dear, I wish we could stay in London. I know I would feel more comfortable here than in Brighton."

"You must have a wedding trip, Belinda."

"I expect I must," Belinda sighed. "It will be so odd being married to a stranger."

Cornelia moved swiftly to Belinda's side and put an arm around her. "My love, you are trembling. You should not be nervous or frightened. He will not be a stranger long. Furthermore, you have seen him quite often in the last weeks."

Belinda moved away from her, and crossing to the window she stood there staring down, but looking at nothing in particular.

"Cornelia," she said finally, "as you are well

aware, I see him on Sundays. He arrives just in time to escort me to church so we may hear the banns read. After the service, he escorts me home. Then, in a half-hour to forty-five minutes, he takes his leave. And, as you also know, we have ridden in the park twice, we have been to Almack's twice, and we have also visited the British Museum. He is very pleasant but I have met other gentlemen who are equally pleasant and who are full of interesting small talk and who pay court to me. He has very little to say for himself, and certainly he does not pay court to me. Seemingly, he has put all that . . . frivolity, if you like, behind him, and his talk is mainly of his home in the country, where he expects that we will stay for part of the year. He discusses whether or not I wish it to be redecorated and whether Mary will come with me or do I need to hire another abigail, and if I should want to hire another abigail, had I better not find her in the country. He *has* talked of Brighton and says that the Prince Regent will be there during our stay, and have I been presented to him. And . . . But I really cannot remember much of his conversation. I am afraid that I have fallen into the regrettable habit of nodding my head and thinking of other things."

"Oh, my dear!" Cornelia exclaimed.

"Exactly." Belinda groaned.

Cornelia said gently, "I cannot but think that when you get to know each other better, you will be extremely compatible."

Belinda gave her a long unhappy look. "I do

not anticipate a lifetime of quarrels, certainly.
Rather than that, I think he will probably be
as indifferent as Papa is with Mama. And she
with him."

"I myself will hope for the best, and I am
sure that in the long run I will not be disappointed," Cornelia said stubbornly.

A group of onlookers, alerted by notices in
the *Morning Post* and the London *Times*, were
gathered near the entrance to the Church of
St. James's in Piccadilly. They had been arriving for close on two hours, and now that
the clock that was set just below the weather
vane on the tall steeple indicated that the
hour was ten minutes before twelve, they
were eagerly anticipating the arrival of the
bride.

Their vigilance was, at length, rewarded by
the appearance of a dark blue coach with a
golden crest painted on the door. It pulled to
a stop in front of the church and a footman
in blue with gold epaulets and quantities of
gold braid on his livery opened the door, bowing as a tall, stylishly dressed gentleman of
some forty-odd years helped the bride to de-
scend. There was an appreciative murmur as
the girl appeared. Though she was veiled,
she was seen to be slim and her gown drew
sighs of envy from the assembled females.
Then, though it was a warm June day, an
obliging breeze blew her veil to one side, re-
vealing a lovely if sober countenance.

"Oooh, she be beautiful," one woman murmured.

"Aye," agreed her companion, a rakish young man. "A sweet armful, right enough, Lil."

He received a sharp tap on the arm with a folded fan and a hissed, "Hush 'Erbert."

"She don't seem very 'appy," whispered another woman. "Maybe because she's marryin' a man old enough to be 'er pa."

"Good gracious, Margaret, 'e 'as to be 'er pa. 'E's got 'er same colorin', red 'air'n I'd lay ye a monkey that she's got 'is green eyes."

"Tha's right, 'e couldn't be nobody else'n look 'oo's comin' now." Another young man pointed. " 'E'll be the groom unless I misses my guess. Rich by the look o' 'im, but 'e could be goin' to 'is own 'angin' rather than 'is weddin'."

" 'Tisn't a marriage made in 'eaven, I'll be bound."

These comments, offered in voices loud enough to be heard by both the bride and her approaching groom, caused that unhappy pair to lock glances and smile, albeit ruefully. Then they hurried into the church and went in different directions, the groom toward a group of youthful officers, members of his regiment home on leave, and the bride lingering with her father as they were approached by a heavy-set gentleman in a white uniform which emphasized his considerable girth.

"Ah, Devereux," the newcomer said cordially. "Well met, man, we do not see you often enough these days."

"Sire, you do me great honor," Lord Devereux said respectfully as he glanced at his

daughter, who had fallen into a deep curtsy.
As she rose, he said, "I do not believe that
you have been presented to his highness, my
dear. My daughter Belinda, sire."

"But she is beautiful," the Prince Regent
said appreciatively as he bent to kiss her hand.
"It seems to me, my dear, that you have much
the look of your mother. Would she be with
you, Devereux?"

Lord Devereux shook his head. "She is not
well, sire."

The Prince appeared regretful. "I am indeed
sorry to hear it. A charming lady. My mother
is particularly fond of her. You will give her
our best wishes for her quick recovery."

"I will convey them to her, sire, as soon as I
return home."

"Ah . . . and do I see young Courtenay? I
must greet him." The Prince smiled and
withdrew.

"It is a shame that Mama had to be ill,"
Belinda said ruefully. "And at such a time."

"You can place her illness at your sister
Pansy's door. It was she who contracted the
quinsy that laid your mother low." He frowned,
adding, "though I am inclined to believe that
she is also under the delusion that it is fash-
ionable to be ailing." His frown vanished as
several other friends hurried to greet him.

"Ah, here you are, and your bridesmaids
over there awaiting you, my dear Belinda."
Cornelia, who had come in Lady Elizabeth's
coach, hurried to Belinda's side. She was smiling tremulously as she added, "Do you know,
my dearest, I would have another white gown

made. You have no notion how becoming it is!"

"I would still have preferred to wear green," Belinda commented.

"Oh, you, I believe you were born contrary!" Cornelia scolded. She added, "I saw Lord Courtenay come in. He is certainly very handsome."

"Someone among the people outside the church said he looked like he was going to a hanging," Belinda told her.

"I am sure that they said a great many things, and all of them of equal import!" Cornelia retorted sarcastically.

"Ah, here you are, my dear, and Lady Cornelia too."

Both girls looked up to find Lord Furneaux standing at their side. He looked incredibly handsome in the understated garments advocated by Beau Brummell, Belinda thought. His cravat was neither too high nor too low, and it was not heavily starched. His coat was dark blue and his pantaloons were buff-colored and strapped under his shining black boots. He was carrying his top hat in one hand, and his dark curls were carefully combed. His rather rueful expression, Belinda thought, could probably be attributed to sad memories of his own nuptials. Actually, those would have been happy memories, so he was probably thinking of the brief span of that marriage. She was realistic enough not to interpret it as regret over her approaching marriage.

If he had ever entertained an idea of offering for her, he must have acted upon it, given his firmness of character. Unfortunately, since he had known her during most of her life, she feared that he still regarded her as the little girl he had both cuddled and teased. She said, "Good day, Lord Furneaux, I am delighted to see you here."

He raised his eyebrows. "You seem surprised, my dear. Did you imagine I would not be present to see you wed, Belinda?" He gave her a warm, affectionate smile.

"I hoped you would come," she replied, stifling a sigh.

"And, lo, those hopes are realized, my dear." His smile broadened. "Might I tell you that you are looking extraordinarily beautiful? A vision of loveliness, in fact. However, is it not time that you were with your bridesmaids?"

"I have come to fetch her for that very purpose, my lord," Cornelia explained.

"I might have guessed that." He turned toward her, and bowing, brought her hand to his lips. As he released it he said, "Might I tell you that you, too, are looking very lovely, Lady Cornelia?"

"You are kind to say so, my lord," she murmured, flushing slightly.

"I beg to differ with you, Lady Cornelia, I am not being at all kind. I am merely being honest."

Before she could reply, a frowning Lady Elizabeth had descended upon them, saying crossly, "Cornelia! Belinda! Why are you tarrying here, pray? Do you not know that it lacks but three minutes of the hour? It is time and past for the procession to form—

have neither of you any sense of the occasion?" She clapped her hands. "Come, come, come, both of you. And where in blazes is your father?"

"He was over there." Belinda, turning, saw Lord Devereux conversing animatedly with a strikingly beautiful young woman. He was looking at her in a way that appeared curiously intimate, and she was smiling at him adoringly, one slender hand on his sleeve.

"Oh, good Lord in heaven," Lady Elizabeth groaned. "And your mother ill in the country! Does the man have no notion of what is fitting and proper?"

Belinda, staring at the couple, said slowly, "Is . . . is she, then, Papa's mistress?"

"Hold your tongue, you little fool!" Lady Elizabeth glared at her.

"I will fetch your father, my dear," Lord Furneaux said smoothly.

"Dearest," Cornelia urged, "do come with us."

"And hurry," Lady Elizabeth snapped, and strode toward the north portal, motioning to the girls to follow her.

"I did not know about Papa," Belinda whispered to Cornelia as they hurried after her. "Do you suppose that is why Mama elected to be ill?"

"Shhhh," Cornelia cautioned nervously. "It is not unusual, you know, my dear. Many gentlemen have mistresses. It has nothing to do with their wives."

"I wonder if Gerald has a mistress," Belinda said thoughtfully.

"If he ever had one, I am sure he does not have one now," Cornelia said firmly.

Belinda fixed a measuring glance on her friend. "Cornelia," she said suspiciously, "I think you know something about Lord Courtenay that I do not."

Cornelia stared at her blankly. "I cannot think what you mean!" she exclaimed.

"Have you heard that he has a mistress?" Belinda pursued doggedly. "I would not mind, you know. In fact, I hope he does."

"Be-lin-da!" Cornelia breathed.

"I really would not mind at all."

"Here we are," Cornelia said thankfully as they neared the whispering, giggling group of bridesmaids.

"Do you expect he would tell me were I to ask him?" Belinda managed to say before they joined the others.

"You will *not* ask him," Cornelia said with uncharacteristic fierceness. "You must *promise* me that you will not ask him."

Belinda was spared a response as Lady Elizabeth joined them, looking very angry. "I don't know what to say . . . I really do not know what to say," she hissed. "No matter, take your places and let's have done."

As the procession formed, the bride was wondering if her father had ceased his conversation with the girl who was, in all probability, his mistress. A second later, he was at her side. She was surprised to find him there so quickly and she was even more surprised when she found herself at the altar. She had no idea how they had managed to get there without her noticing it, but she was standing next to her bridegroom and facing the elderly Anglican minister whose sermons had bored her every Sunday since her arrival in London. A quick look at Gerald showed her that he looked as handsome as ever—but not, to her mind, as handsome as Lord Furneaux. A sigh threatened and she hastily swallowed it. It did not do to sigh over him. He did not care for her, and given his eternal mourning, it did not really matter whom she married. She was quite positive that she would never love anyone else.

Indeed, it was just as well that she was marrying Gerald. They would soon be on their way to Brighton, and at least she would not be constantly seeing Lord Furneaux at one or another rout or ball or at the theater. If she did not see him, perhaps one day in the far future she would be able to stop thinking about him. With that enviable condition in mind, she spoke her responses firmly, much more firmly than her groom. A quick glance at his face showed her that he was not looking very happy. Probably he did have a mistress, she decided. She suddenly felt very sorry for him. In a sense, they did have a great deal in common, though she strongly doubted that it was what their parents had anticipated when they had so arbitrarily ordered the match.

Once the wedding was over, the young couple were borne out of the church by their excited friends and relations. The destination of the wedding party was Lady Elizabeth's home. She had requested and had been gladly accorded the dubious honor of providing the reception and a substantial repast for fifty-odd guests, including the bride's father and the groom's parents.

Lord and Lady Courtenay had arrived during the ceremony with audible excuses and muttered comments concerning the deplorable state of roads rutted by a recent rain and the regrettable inability of their footmen and outriders to change a stone-shattered carriage wheel in less than an hour. It was a mishap that had left them badly shaken, and Lady Courtenay complained that her head was aching and would doubtless continue aching for days. They discussed their resulting fright and attendant fears that they might miss the ceremony in low voices while their son and daughter-in-law-to-be exchanged their vows. Afterward they recounted the whole of it to Lord Devereux, once they arrived at the reception, while he explained the reason for the absence of his lady.

Meanwhile, the newly married pair circulated among the assembled company, the bride being kissed by her bridesmaids and the groom being congratulated by his friends, his relations, and his parents. If neither Belinda nor Gerald exchanged so much as a word, no one save a watchful and concerned Lady Cornelia appeared to be aware of it—at least that was what she had hopefully believed until she found herself confronted by a frowning Lord Furneaux. His brow cleared as he looked down at her.

"Lady Cornelia, well met," he murmured.

"My Lord Furneaux," she responded with a breathlessness that she immediately deplored and prayed that he had not noticed. To cover that unfortunate condition, she added hastily, "It was a lovely ceremony, was it not?"

His frown returned. "I am not sure that it was," he said frankly. "And furthermore, my dear Lady Cornelia, I have a strong suspicion that you know what I mean." Before she could reply, he continued doggedly, "I have long regretted these arbitrary couplings which do not take into account the preferences of either party."

"Oh, I am in complete agreement!" Cornelia exclaimed, startled into frankness by his unexpected admission. "Poor Belinda begged to be released from the obligations imposed upon her by her parents."

"I am sure she did," he said rather grimly. "I understand that she scarcely knows him."

"That is true," Cornelia agreed indignantly. Ruefully she proceeded to explain the circumstances attendant upon the bride's initial encounter with the groom. She had anticipated a lightening of his mood and possibly laughter, but he continued sober.

"Five and eleven," he said thoughtfully. "Well, my dear, they are, in a sense, more fortunate than those in other centuries. I expect you are aware that two or three hundred years ago girls of five and even younger were wed, sometimes by proxy, to boys of eleven or twelve, and separated until they were believed old enough to assume the obligations of marriage. We have progressed beyond that point, but to my notion, further progress is certainly warranted."

"To mine also." She nodded. "Marriage certainly ought to be based on more than mere financial considerations." She might have enlarged more upon that theme, but at that moment Lord Furneaux was hailed by a crony who insistently drew him away to meet a languishing female on the other side of the chamber.

She looked after his retreating figure with a sense of strong regret. With Belinda gone, it was unlikely that she would see him again. In fact, she had a definite feeling that his fulminations against forced marriage might be based on a possible penchant for her friend. It was also possible that he was not even aware of his feelings, and she wished that she were in that same enviable condition. Unfortunately, she had fallen in love with Lord Furneaux in practically the same moment they had been introduced, and since that introduction had been made at a ball in Edinburgh last year, she was gloomily aware that even without the proper nourishment, her love was a hardy perennial that could exist even in the desert.

"Cornelia!" Belinda hurried to her side, effectively scattering her unwelcome reminiscences. "Lord Courtenay says that we must leave immediately if we are to be in Brighton by noon tomorrow! His father has told us that it was very difficult to make reservations at the Ship Hotel and that the proprietor told him that they would not be held beyond one in the afternoon. He is quite exercised over the matter . . . but I will not go into all that." She lowered her voice. "I really do not like him and I certainly do not like her!"

"Who might 'her' be, my dear?" Cornelia inquired.

"Lady Courtenay . . ." Belinda grimaced. "She is extremely toplofty and I feel that she looks down on *me*, though I cannot imagine why."

"Ah." Cornelia smiled wryly. "You are encountering a mother-in-law. My mama was burdened by one of the species for a great deal of her married life—though she withdrew to the country after Papa died, and badgered Aunt Cecilia, her eldest unmarried daughter, instead. Now that your husband is an *only* son . . . But I will not refine upon it longer, save to tell you that Mama used to nod agreement to all that Grandmama told her and then do exactly as she pleased."

Belinda laughed. "Fortunately, I do not believe that I will be forced to such stratagems. The Courtenays will not be living with us. We will be residing in London, as you know, and Gerald has told me that his parents loathe the city." She paused and then added unhappily, "I do wish you were coming with us today."

Cornelia put an arm around Belinda's shoulders. "My dear, I am of the opinion that you will find you have all the companionship you will need—on this particular journey." Meeting her friend's doubtful gaze, she contin-

ued, determinedly hiding her own doubts,
"Once you are better acquainted, I am sure
you will deal together most felicitously."

She received another, even more doubtful
look from Belinda. "Well, if we do not, there
is Brighton. I have been longing to see the
town and I have never swum in the ocean."

"I have, and found it most exhilarating,"
Cornelia said bracingly.

A short time later, followed by Cornelia and
her other bridesmaids, and with more reas-
surances ringing in her ears, Belinda hurried
upstairs to be divested of her wedding gown
and helped into a new walking dress of green
cambric muslin worn with a dark green spen-
cer. Her hat, also green, was close-fitting and
decorated with a white ostrich plume. In other
circumstances she would have been delighted
by the costume, since the green seemed to
make her eyes appear even greener and since
it also complimented her auburn curls, but
the wide gold band on her third finger, left
hand, robbed the occasion of its pleasure. In
fact, as she came down the stairs, she strongly
wished herself a hundred miles distant.

Unfortunately, that wish, in common with
so many of her wishes, could not be granted.
She joined her husband and tried to forget
the prurient conversation in the bedroom regarding the unfolding mysteries of the married state and offered in the name of advice
by several of her bridesmaids. Much to her
regret, these whispered, giggling confidences
continued to circulate through her mind as
Lord Courtenay helped her into the waiting

coach. In fact, she had a wild desire to slide quickly across that cushioned seat and out the other door, disappearing among the crowds that thronged the street, many of the pedestrians halting to stare at the wedding party. Still, if she had learned anything from her governess at home and her teachers at school, it was that young women in her exalted position did not heed the wild promptings of impulse, particularly not this impulse!

She must remember that she was now Lady Courtenay and that the heady excitement of her first London Season was a thing of the past. From now on she must accept the responsibilities attendant upon her new position. A side glance at his lordship's handsome profile brought her an impression of tenseness and of a smile that appeared and disappeared—suggesting that he was of a similar mind and no happier than herself.

Then, much sooner than Belinda liked, the carriage drew away. She waved at her assembled friends while she scanned the crowd for a glimpse of Lord Furneaux, whom she had seen earlier, but only at a distance, and then speaking with Cornelia! She remembered being beset by a most regrettable feeling of jealousy. Then she did see him, and he was not anywhere near Cornelia. He was standing on the corner staring into a space which, though it included her carriage, did not, she decided, include her. She sighed and turned her head, and in so doing encountered her husband's gaze. Again she had a feeling that he did not really see her—and who occupied

his mind's eye? She was sure that it was a
woman who had occasioned that yearning
look. Had it been one of the females at the
church or at the reception? Possibly the lady
in question had been at both places.

That such speculations were hardly those a
new bride should entertain did not trouble
one whose heart remained behind, firmly held
in the careless or, rather, uncaring clutch of
Lord Furneaux. He could not mourn his wife
forever, she thought resentfully. Then her resentment turned to anguish as she reminded
herself that she could never be the one who
might help banish the persistent image of
the late Lady Furneaux from his heart and
mind.

On his side of the coach, Lord Courtenay,
alternately smiling and waving to his father
and his friends, was resenting the earl with
all his heart. Indeed, though he was certainly
not pleased with his present company or at
the thought of his destination, he was glad
he would not need to see his parents for some
time. They were returning to the family castle, where they lived most of the year. They
would not join him and his bride in the London house. Having neatly ruined his life, they
would continue to mourn for Edward, whom
they much preferred to him. He was reasonably sure that if Edward had not wanted to
marry Belinda, they would have acceded to
his request. Edward could do no wrong. Edward . . . But it was useless and wrong to
dwell on poor Edward. There was another

who should occupy his thoughts at present—
his bride.

He turned a groan into a cough and continued to stare out of the window, waving to
his friends. Still, he must eventually try to
work up some semblance of enthusiasm for
his bride. It had been easier when he had
seen her only briefly. What would he say to
her now? . . . Indeed, what could he say to
her during the days and days and days they
would need to spend together?

At this moment it was useless to try to find
an answer to this question. He could compare his situation to that of a soldier about
to confront an enemy about whom he had
been told nothing. Of course, Belinda was
not an enemy, but certainly she was an unknown quantity and no more enthusiastic
regarding their marriage than himself, poor
child! Rather than resenting her presence,
he should try to be kind to her. If they could
never be lovers, they might eventually be
friends.

With that in mind, he turned toward her
and was relieved to find her still staring out
of the window as the equipage moved forward down the street. Words were evidently
not needed now. Later . . . But he would not
dwell on "later." He would settle back and
think of something pleasant or, rather, someone. *Felice.*

"Brighton!" Belinda muttered, and groaned
as she gazed from the window of her hotel to
the shining stretch of sea that lay beyond the

brown-pebbled beaches of that famous resort.
There was a small ship in the distance or,
rather, it appeared small from her window, a
toy boat on a vast pond. She turned her eyes
in another direction and saw the bathing machines, actually tall wooden boxes on small
platforms, drawn by elderly mules that plod-
ded down into the sea, where brawny females,
called dippers, waited to immerse bathers in
the chilly salt water. She grimaced, unwill-
ingly remembering the moment when she had
first approached them.

It had been on the afternoon of their arrival and she had gladly left the suite of rooms
reserved by her father-in-law to find something that might keep her away from her
husband for at least two hours. She would
have preferred that time to be extended to
four or even twenty-four hours, she remembered wryly. She loved to swim and had often
swum in the large lake on their property in
Lincolnshire. Consequently, the thought of a
dip in the ocean had been singularly appeal-
ing on that hot July afternoon. Unfortunately,
she learned to late that the bathers who used
the machines did not swim. Instead, the dippers, keeping a tight hold on them, pushed
them down into the waves, holding them so
they were in no danger of being dragged out
to sea by one or another breaker.

She, however, had determinedly eluded
them, and ignoring their rough protests, had
swum out beyond the breakers, defiantly remaining there as long as she chose, which as
it happened, proved to be far too long. She

had become chilled, and that very night she had caught the quinsy, which had kept her bedded for the last five days. Another cough racked her and she wondered how Gerald was faring. Hard on that thought, there was a knock on their connecting door.

"Yes?" she called hoarsely.

Gerald opened the door. He was clad in a vividly patterned brocade dressing robe over a flannel nightshirt. He stared at her out of reddened eyes. His nose was also red from constant applications of his handkerchief. "Are you feeling more the thing, my dear?" he croaked.

"No," Belinda coughed. "And nor are you, I expect."

He said ruefully, "I imagine that being in Spain so long, the heat of the country thinned my blood, else I cannot believe that this quinsy would have seized such hold of me."

"Again, I apologize for staying in the water so long."

"It was a pleasant day," he said. "And after such indifferent roads, the sea . . ." He sneezed. "I am sure it must have seemed extremely inviting to you."

"It did," she said feelingly, glad that he could not read her mind and learn that one of the temptations offered by the sea was protection. Earlier that fatal day, it had seemed to Belinda that he was looking at her in a strange, speculative way—as if he were trying to make up his mind about something. She had feared that that something might concern that mysterious process by which they would become one—the ramifications of which neither her Aunt Elizabeth nor her father had thought to divulge to her. She had expected that she might receive that knowledge when they stopped for the night at the Red Lion Inn on the way to Brighton. However, Gerald had told her that he was extremely weary, and having heard from her that she was in a similar state of exhaustion, he had thankfully bidden her a hasty good night and hurried to his chamber. She, much relieved, had retired to her bed in the adjoining room—much to the confusion of Mary, who, by looks and clicks of her tongue, had managed to convey a continuing confusion heavily laced with disapproval.

"Would you mind, my dear," Gerald said, bringing her back to the present, "if we . . . we . . ." He began to cough.

Waiting patiently until the paroxysm passed, Belinda said, "What were you about to tell me?"

"Would you mind if we were to return to London? I . . . I find that I am not really enjoying the sea air."

Obviously, in common with herself, poor Gerald could not even smell the sea air. She said gladly, "Oh, nor am I. Do you really wish to return to London?"

"Indeed, I do, and as soon as possible."

"Today?" she asked eagerly.

He sighed. "I wish to might be today, but I believe it would be better were we to leave first thing in the morning."

"I will be ready anytime you choose!" she

said happily, and then inwardly quailed as her husband gave her what might almost be interpreted as a loving look. Fortunately, another racking cough shook him and he hurried back to his chamber, probably for a draft of that ill-tasting medicine the doctor had given him. She hoped it would grant him some surcease from the agony which she, all unwittingly, had thrust upon him.

As the large traveling coach rolled back into bustling, overcrowded, and warm London, Belinda, a handkerchief to her nose in anticipation of the sneezing which had marked her passage from Sussex and through most of Kent, looked almost fondly on her husband's house. Though she would have much preferred returning to her Aunt Elizabeth's home, preferred being Lady Belinda Devereux rather than Courtenay, the fact that the house in question was located in London, even a London sweltering under an unusually hot sun, was enough to bring a smile to her mouth and an answering glint to her eyes.

In this same city, Lord Furneaux also resided. Then, too, there was her dear friend Cornelia, whom she had truly missed. It was very difficult not having someone in whom she could confide. In fact, she had never felt so utterly alone as in these, the first days of marriage. Certainly, she did not feel in the least married.

A racking cough from the man beside her served to remind her that feelings or no feelings, she was bound to him. She turned swiftly, "I expect that your health must improve now that we are back in London."

"I . . . I . . ." Another racking cough shook him. "I hope so," he rasped. "Imagine to . . . to go safely through a thousand odd skirmishes with the damned French and . . . and then to be laid low with this blasted quinsy. Damn, but I feel as weak as a cat!"

"Oh, dear, that is a pity." Despite her increasing pleasure at being once more in London, Belinda did feel sorry for her stricken lord. She guessed that, given his strong constitution, he had very little patience with illness and, indeed, she was sure that he was rarely ill. "I feel that your misery must be laid at my door," she said contritely.

"Nonsense, my dear." He reached out a hand to pat her on the shoulder, but took it back hastily to pluck his handkerchief from his pocket and stifle another threatening sneeze.

"You must go to bed as soon as we reach the house," Belinda said.

"I will. . . ." He regarded her through red, tearing eyes. "I . . . I am sorry about all this. It cannot be very pleasant for you, especially now that you are practically recovered. For your sake, I wish we might have remained in Brighton."

Since the truth could hardly have pleased him, Belinda contented herself with saying, "I am sure you will soon be recovered too, G-Gerald." She flushed, wishing that she had not stuttered. Until recently she had addressed him as "my lord," but he had protested this formality, saying sharply that they were married and had not to stand on ceremony. When she reminded him that some ladies of rank never used their husbands' given names, he had replied that he did not hold with that convention. She had not dared to explain that she preferred that convention, because it would have necessitated yet another explanation, which, of course, she would not have dared to provide.

Indeed, how might she tell him that she feared that the relaxing of one convention would bring them closer together and that would result in what her aunt had called "marital duties"? Lady Elizabeth had not explained the nature of these duties, but Belinda, picking up bits of information from her friends, guessed that they entailed intimacies which, more often than not, resulted in the birth of a child. Though she was fully aware that that was why she had been married, she did not want to bear a child immediately. She wanted . . . The image of Lord Furneaux flickered in her mind's eye and, of a sudden, she was sure that if he had been her husband, she would not have been frightened of those intimacies.

Gerald was shaken by another cough, one that effectively banished her convoluted thoughts. "Oh, dear," she said. "I will be glad when we arrive. I am sure that the attentions of your physician will make all the difference."

"I hope so," he said gloomily. He added, "Mrs. Forsythe, the housekeeper, will see that you are made comfortable, my dear. Ah," he added in some surprise, "we are here."

Looking out of the window, Belinda found that the carriage had stopped in front of a massive house fronted by high wrought-iron gates. A flagstone path lying between clipped hedges ended at a pillared portico. She liked the fact that the house was set back from the street and that beyond the hedges lay wide lawns. Yet, once she was out of the coach and standing before an oak door centered by a knocker in the shape of a snarling lion, Belinda found the effect more intimidating than welcoming. Or was it that she herself did not feel welcome? There was yet another interpretation to be placed on her feelings, and that was an almost overwhelming desire to return to her aunt's house and be Belinda Devereux again. Fortunately, before she could dwell too long on that particular feeling, they were inside the mansion, being greeted by Thomas, the butler, and by Mrs. Forsythe, the housekeeper. Both servants seemed caught between surprise and concern as Gerald, leaning heavily on his valet's arm, came slowly into the hall and sank down gratefully on a bench just beyond the entrance.

"But what is this, Master Gerald?" the housekeeper demanded almost sternly, as if, indeed, she were scolding him, Belinda thought.

Gerald answered with a sneeze. "I . . . I am not at my best, Mrs. Forsythe," he murmured. "This blasted quinsy . . ."

"Aye, and it's easy to see that it has taken a strong hold of you," she said more sympathetically, but still with that odd note in her voice that reminded Belinda most unpleasantly of Mrs. Murray, a particularly strict nurse who had cared for her and her brothers and sisters when they were little. In fact, she seemed far more like a nurse than a housekeeper. Her eyes matched her voice, being a glacial gray, and then, as that gray gaze turned in her direction, she found herself more than ever reminded of Mrs. Murray, who had ruled her charges with an iron hand and, on many occasions, a stout switch.

She instinctively braced herself, but managed to say coolly enough, "I think it best if my husband were to retire immediately, Mrs. Forsythe. It has been a strenuous journey for someone in his condition."

"My dear," Gerald said hastily, "Mrs. Forsythe will do what is necessary." Belatedly he added, "I fear I have been remiss. This is Mrs. Forsythe, who was once the nurse of my brother and myself and who has now taken over the duties of housekeeper. And this, Mrs. Forsythe, is the Lady Belinda, my wife."

"Aye, I know that." The housekeeper sketched a curtsy. "It's welcome you are, milady, and welcomed you ought to have been before this—save that Master Gerald's took all our attention, being so poorly. And sure your orders will be carried out. I have had his bed opened and I have already sent one of the lads for the doctor. Meanwhile, you'd best have a bit of a rest yourself. You look fair wrung out, child."

The smile that accompanied her words softened Mrs. Forsythe's grim face and her com-

ments served to banish Belinda's incipient
animosity. She said gratefully, "I . . . I do
find myself a little wearied from the journey."

"She is not only wearied from the journey,"
Gerald said. "She, too, has been afflicted with
this same ailment. I hope you received my
letter regarding household arrangements."

"I did that, Master Gerald. And your mother
has directed that her ladyship rest in her
chambers."

He nodded. "I thought she would agree to
that." He turned to Belinda, giving her a brief
smile. "My parents have never enjoyed living
in London. I have a strong notion that they
mean to remain in the country. If you hanker
for country life, we can either visit them at
the castle or we may go to York, where I have
another property."

"I really do enjoy the city," Belinda assured
him hastily.

He appeared to be much relieved. "As do I,
my dear. We are quite agreed on that."

The chambers that had once been occupied by Gerald's mother were hung in white
and gold. They consisted of a commodious
bedchamber, a good-size sitting room, and a
dressing room with a prettily tiled adjoining
bathroom with running water, thus abolish-
ing the need for watering cans of a morning.
A door in the bedroom proved to be locked,
and this, the housekeeper explained, led into
Gerald's dressing room and thence to his
bedchamber.

Once she was alone, Belinda eyed that portal
nervously and guessed that the key was in

Gerald's possession. Judging from his prior actions, she was rather sure that the door would remain locked. Certainly she did not regret that. In fact, it was an ideal situation for one who had no desire to plumb the mysteries of marriage and who believed herself well on the way to being in love with a gentleman who was not her husband.

It little mattered that Lord Furneaux had given her no encouragement. She had been a young unmarried female during all the years she had known him. Now that situation was changed. She was married, and to a husband who was no more interested in her than she in him. Having heard somewhere—she did not remember how or when—that gentlemen believed it great sport and quite safe to flirt with married females, she did hope that Lord Furneaux was of their number. After all, she reasoned hopefully, he could not grieve forever.

3

On a warm day in late August, the rooms of Hardy, Howell & Company, Ltd., located on busy Pall Mall, were even warmer by reason of the crowds of females thronging them. The vast store offered an abundance of costly temptations to its eager customers. There were no fewer than five different boutiques on the ground floor—these given over to fans, furs, hats, jewelry, and gloves. Another room was devoted to yard goods, and many items were either imported or smuggled in from France. Indeed, there was even furniture to be had in another part of the building, which had once been a ducal mansion.

In addition to these amenities, there was Mr. Conway's Breakfast Room, called after a former tenant of the mansion, and offering hungry shoppers refreshments and more sturdy meals as well.

It was to this particular room, with its windows facing a stretch of London from St. James's Park to Westminister, and with the Surrey hills in the distance, that Belinda had come to take tea with Cornelia and gaze at that entrancing view. At least Belinda appeared to find the view entrancing. Cornelia's eyes were on her friend, her transformed friend.

In the five times she had seen her since her return from Brighton, she had yet to find Belinda wearing the same gown. At present, mindful of the August weather, she was wearing a walking dress of white muslin, frilled at the hem and at the throat. A beautiful Indian shawl with long green fringe was draped over her shoulders, and her little kid slippers were black in deference to London's dirty streets—not that she did much walking on them. Her smart new cabriolet, with its spirited horse and its youthful but highly experienced groom in the green livery of Lord Courtenay's house, was waiting below. As usual, she seemed in the best of spirits and she was animatedly telling Cornelia about the set of cameos her husband had purchased for her for no other reason than he thought they must become her.

In fact, clothes and jewels had been her main topic of conversation. She had just purchased several lengths of silk and one of Indian muslin and, over Cornelia's strong protests, she had insisted on providing her with a length of blue-gray silk, which she insisted was almost a perfect match for her eyes. By dint of saying that she did not like a certain gold necklace, Cornelia had prevented her friend from buying it for her. Belinda was still arguing with Cornelia about it.

"I assure you that Gerald will not mind. He

does not care how much I spend. I could have a new gown for every day of the year. He just turns my bills over to his man of business, and as you know, my allowance is huge! I am having a ball gown made of . . . Which reminds me, my dear, why did I not see you at the Grosvenor Ball last Tuesday? You will not tell me that you lacked an invitation, for I know that the marchioness is very fond of you."

Cornelia smiled at her. "My love, unlike yourself, I do not have the stamina to go out every night, and besides, your aunt might not like it. After all, I am her guest."

"But she does not force you to be her companion. I know that for a fact. I have a feeling that she hopes you will find a husband here. You ought to be married, my dear."

"I wonder if I will ever be married," Cornelia mused. "I do not have a large portion, as you know."

"I will be glad to increase it," Belinda said quickly. "I wish you would let me do it. I assure you that Gerald would not mind. He, too, is fond of you, and besides that, he is as rich as Midas."

"I have said I will not take it, and there's an end to it," Cornelia responded firmly.

"But it is not charity." Belinda frowned. "It is because you are my very best friend and I love you. Please, Cornelia, be sensible and accept it."

"No, my darling. Did you enjoy yourself at Almack's last night?"

"Oh." Belinda shrugged. "I expect I did.

Gerald danced with me only once because I was surrounded as soon as I entered the ballroom. I expect that if I had not written his name down on a spoke of my fan before I appeared on the floor, he would not have been vouchsafed a single dance."

"Ah, another triumph!"

"Nonsense!" Belinda said crossly. "I do not count dances with a lot of silly young men and boring older ones a triumph. I am beginning to think that I do not really care for balls and such. They are only interesting if . . . if you meet people you find interesting and who do not fill your head with a lot of silly compliments which mean nothing! Which reminds me, I have not seen Lord Furneaux in the last fortnight . . . I expect that he has gone to the country."

"No, he is in town. He came to call on Lady Elizabeth the day before yesterday?"

"Oh, did he?" Belinda said after a slight pause. "Were you present to greet him?"

Cornelia shook her head and said with the suggestion of a sigh, "No, I was having tea with Maria Craven. I expect you remember her from school?"

Belinda shook her head. "No. I only remember you from school. We two against the world, do you recall that? We were both so serious. I was going to write books and you were going to paint pictures. Neither of us gave a thought to marriage—and lo and behold, in my very first Season . . . and that not even ended yet, I am Lady Courtenay, with rings on my fingers and bells on my toes!"

Cornelia, who had been looking concerned, appeared even more concerned as Belinda ceased speaking. "My darling," she said softly, "why do I believe you unhappy?"

Belinda raised her eyebrows. "I really cannot understand you, Cornelia, dearest. How can you imagine that I am unhappy? I have become very popular, my love. My desk is piled high with invitations. If I answered only half of them, I would be occupied until 1820! Of course, that is an exaggeration, but really, marriage unlocks a great many doors. You are no longer a threat, you see. And, at the same time, you are beset with temptations which could ruin you—were you not of firm character. I have discovered that it is extremely pleasurable to let one or another tempter believe you tempted . . . and then, just as he is sure that he has you tangled in his net, you produce a scissors from your reticule and cut your way out. Those nets are made of spun gossamer or, possibly, they are woven by spiders."

"Belinda, you are talking of nothing!" Cornelia protested.

" 'True, I talk of dreams which are the children of an idle brain. Begot of nothing but vain fantasy . . .' Ah, now, there's a writer for you—Shakespeare."

"And what of your own writing?" Cornelia frowned.

"And what of it? Would you expect me to continue with it now that I am married?" Belinda asked in a hard little voice.

"Why would you not?"

"I was writing romances, was I not? Well, let us say that I have ceased to believe in romances. And if I cannot believe in them, how is it possible to write about them? Besides, as I think I have already hinted, I have so much to do, and between the much, there is more. I am allowed to make some changes in the house. Gerald has been kind enough to trust me with the task. He finds my taste in garments to his liking. I will soon be visiting furniture houses . . . Will you come with me? I do hope so."

"If you wish, I will, of course," Cornelia said. "But to get back to your writing, my dear—"

"My writing is no more," Belinda interrupted. "And I begin to believe that it was always 'vain fantasy.' "

Belinda was blinking rapidly, Cornelia noted, and then, to her surprise, she saw that her friend's lengthy lashes were wet. "My love, what is amiss?" she exclaimed impulsively. "Why are you so very unhappy?"

The green eyes grew hard. "But I have told you, Cornelia, dear. I am not unhappy. Thanks to the determined efforts of my parents and those of my husband's parents, I am firmly settled in society and I expect that soon I will be required to . . . But enough, Cornelia. Come down and let us go for a drive. Then I will take you home . . . and you will not forget that we are to make merry at Vauxhall Gardens tomorrow night with Gerald and one or another of his friends?"

"I am looking forward to it." Cornelia managed a smile. "Even though your aunt assures me that it is a wicked place."

Belinda laughed. "It is only wicked if you are an unaccompanied female. There are plenty of those about, and I have never heard that they suffered from their wickedness. Come, let us go."

"And so you will take your bride to Vauxhall Gardens, Gerald." Felice smiled up at him.

He laughed. "Yes, because she has heard of its far-from-savory reputation and wishes to see this sink of evil for herself."

"She wishes to see it or to test it?" Felice asked teasingly.

"She will not be able to test it in my presence," Gerald replied a little stiffly.

"You mean you do not intend to give her free rein?" Felice laughed.

"Certainly not! She is an innocent, as I have told you."

Felice nodded. She wound her arms around his neck. "And are you telling me, *mon ami*, that she still remains innocent?"

He frowned. "The situation remains unchanged."

"And after all these weeks, you are not tempted, not at all?"

His frown, having disappeared, reappeared. "Would I be with you every moment that I can snatch?" he inquired hotly. "Would I call you 'my club' or a 'regimental dinner' or a 'meeting with my man of business'? Ever since we returned from Brighton, I have used these excuses. I have pretended relapses, have mentioned headaches. Indeed, there are times when I dislike myself thoroughly for my pretenses, and I am not at all sure that she does not feel the same way."

"If you learn that she does dislike you, Gerald, my dear, what would you do were she to look in other places for amusement and, perhaps, a friend?"

His frowning gaze became a near-glare. "She would not!" he snapped.

"Oh, dear, I have made you angry, I fear." Felice sighed. "Why are we discussing these matters, my love, especially when I know how difficult it is for you to come to me? If I appear discontented with the situation . . . if I tease you a little, you must forgive me. I am not happy either, especially when I remember how very happy we used to be . . . those glorious days when you came home on leave and did not stir from my bed. If you knew how very much I long for those days, my Gerald . . ."

"You cannot long for them any more than I, my beautiful one," he sighed. "I have suggested that she ought to visit her mother, but they are not in sympathy, and while she is fond of her aunt, Lady Elizabeth lives in town."

"And her father . . . I hear he is occasionally in town."

"She is even less in sympathy with him," he said wryly. "She has discovered that he has a mistress who is less than half her mother's age."

"And probably she is aware that you do not care for her either, poor child. Perhaps you should disabuse her mind of that, my dear."

He looked at her in surprise. "You are suggesting that I make love to her?"

"Make love to your wife!" she repeated in mock horror. "Certainly not! That would be unthinkable. No, no, no, I had another suggestion entirely. I think you ought to commission her portrait. I have a friend who is an excellent artist, and he could paint her. He is particularly good at depicting females and he has recently returned from the country, where he painted the Duchess of Millard. If your little wife were to pose for a portrait, it would keep her occupied and less at loose ends. Furthermore, she would be pleased that you desired it."

"Ummmm." He regarded her thoughtfully. "Is this man well-known?"

"He has recently been elected to the Royal Academy and he has gained quite a reputation. He is also French and of the nobility."

"Are there any exiled French who are not of the nobility?" Gerald grinned, an expression that quickly faded when he met Felice's reproachful look. "I am sorry, my dearest, I was only teasing, you know."

She moved away from him. "I cannot speak for all my countrymen," she said stiffly. "But Chrétien d'Angoulême is descended from a line which gave a daughter to the English throne. He is a duke in his own right . . . and this man, who was born to luxury, has lived from hand to mouth until very recently."

"Even though he is a good painter?" Gerald asked, and received another glare from Felice.

"Painters, my love, unless they are the late Sir Joshua Reynolds or George Romney, do not easily win recognition here in London. It would be a great boon for Chrétien were he to paint the bride of a lord. You have friends. They will stroll through the gallery in your house and see his work and—"

"Very well," he interrupted. "I will consider it, but of course I wish to see his paintings. It is not that I do not trust your judgment, my love, but—"

"But of course you must see them," she said quickly. "I would not have it any other way, and nor would Chrétien. You will see his work and you will meet him. By the way, he does not use his family name. He prefers 'de Beaufort.' His painting in the Royal Academy was one he finished last year, using a model. It depicts the Virgin Mary at the well, should you wish to see it."

"Of course I will go, and the more I think of it, the better I like the notion. Belinda ought to have her picture painted. And now . . ." He broke off, smiling at her.

"Et maintenant . . ." she murmured provocatively, and then laughed as he picked her up and effortlessly bore her to her couch.

"Do you not believe we have had enough discussion this day?" he inquired.

Felice nodded her agreement and emphasized it by pulling him down beside her and winding her arms around his neck.

"And so . . ." Chrétien de Beaufort bent a roguish brown eye on Felice. "You have for me a commission, yes? One of your collection of English gentlemen?"

"I do not have a collection." She frowned.

"I know, my love. I was only teasing. We are speaking about your latest lover, I believe?"

"I am speaking about his wife, who is very young, very naive, and virginal besides."

"You say that she gives the suggestion of being a virgin?" he inquired.

"I am saying, Chrétien, that she *is* a virgin, a ripe fruit on the tree of love, my dear, but not yet separated from the bough."

He raised well-shaped brows. "You will never tell me that, Felice!"

"But I do tell you that . . . and more," she responded, and proceeded to do so.

"And does he want her gentled as well as painted?" he asked in some surprise.

Her gaze hardened. "I want it. . . . He does not, and I expect he would run you through were you to do it."

"And why, then, may I ask, do you wish me to thrust my head into this particular lion's mouth?"

Her eyes hardened. "I have my reasons, Chrétien."

"I do not remember . . . have you known this candidate for cuckoldry very long, my dearest?"

"I have known him long enough." Felice frowned. "There was a time when . . . But never mind about that. There is a commission in it, there might be sport and also fame. You are an excellent painter."

"We both know that, but I should not want my excellent heart spitted upon the point of a rapier or punctured by a bullet. At present, I have more expertise with a brush than with either of these weapons."

"I should not imagine that he would wish to proclaim his wife's downfall to the polite world. A duel would generate considerable curiosity amongst the *ton*."

Chrétien visited a long look on her face. "But what is amiss, my dearest Felice?" he asked softly. "I have known you for many years and I have never seen you so vindictive. Has this child done you an injury, then?"

"Let us say that I do not believe that she is above temptation."

"Does he?"

"Indeed, yes, because she is of his exalted class . . . your exalted class, Chrétien. No, I cannot imagine that a heir to an earldom can compare in rank to a duke!"

He shrugged and laughed. "Let us not dwell on empty titles, my dear. What is really troubling you?"

She raised anguished eyes to his face. "He would have married me, Chrétien, save that his brother died and he inherited the title— and his brother's bride."

"Did you love him so much, then?"

She moved away from him. "I cared for him, care for him, but it would have meant much to me to . . . to be respectable."

"Was he aware of that, my dear?"

"No, but he loved me . . . loves me, wants me, wanted me, and would have married me had not his brother died. I know what you will say—I have him yet—but my position remains the same. I was not meant to be a *fille de joie*, Chrétien."

"And you are not!" He strode to her side and drew her into his embrace. "You are a fine artist." He frowned. "Did he offer for you?"

"Yes, he did, and then rescinded it."

"Why do you still see him?" he asked.

"I should not, but I . . . I cannot bring myself to . . . to put an end to everything."

"My poor Felice." He frowned. "You may send him to me and I will let you know the outcome."

"Please," she murmured, half-glad and half-regretful that she had drawn him into her scheme. She wondered if she ought to confess the truth and tell him that Gerald would never have married her, brother or no brother, but as she contemplated that possiblity, he kissed her lightly on the cheek, and blowing her yet another kiss, was out the door.

She came slowly back to her couch and sank down on it, thinking now of Gerald's bride, whom she deeply resented both for her position and for the accident of birth that had made her legitimate and herself illegitimate, the daughter of an artist who painted scenery at the Comédie Française, and the marquess, who had mistaken her mother for an actress. He had cast her aside when he found she was with child. She had returned

to work, and then, terrified by the excesses of
the Revolution, she had fled France and continued to work in the theater—at Covent Garden and in the Italian opera house. She found
lodgings in Marylebone with another artist,
a miniaturist who taught Felice her craft and
when she was thirteen had taken her as his
mistress, over her mother's frantic objections.

Felice had subsequently learned that she
had usurped her mother's place in his affections. When she could afford it, she left him
and struck out on her own. There had been
other lovers, but Gerald . . . Gerald she loved
only a little less than Chrétien, whose casual
caresses she coveted. Still, Chrétien, despite
his poverty, might one day regain his title
and . . . But she did not want to think about
Chrétien. It was better to have him as a friend.
A friend who would teach Gerald a needed
lesson.

Faced with the young man whose talents
Felice had praised so highly, Gerald regarded
him narrowly. Despite Felice's description of
him, Chrétien de Beaufort was not what he
had expected. Though he was clad in garments which had certainly seen better days,
the man had a natural elegance. He was also
handsome and, indeed, it was not hard to
believe that he was one of those noblemen
who had fled France. Furthermore, the painting Gerald had seen in the Academy certainly
attested to his talent.

Ending a conversation that had revolved
around price, Gerald said, "I think it were

better were you to paint my wife in our home.
I do not like to think of her coming all the
way to Chelsea, even though she would have
an abigail with her."

"I quite understand, my lord," the artist
replied. "It is, however, to be hoped that you
have in your house a chamber that will provide me with a north light?"

"We do. The library faces north," Gerald
said. "Would you mind working there?"

"I would not mind in the least, my lord, if
there is the light I require."

"I assure you that there is, and possibly a
shelf of books would be an excellent back-
ground for my wife, since she fancies herself
a novelist."

"Ah, she, too, is an artist?" Chrétien asked
interestedly.

"I would not know about that, Monsieur de
Beaufort. I have not read her work."

"I see."

Hearing a faint intonation of surprise in
the artist's voice, Gerald flushed and added
defensively, "It is not from any lack of interest on my part. She has not shown any of her
efforts to me. I have the impression that she
is shy about her writing."

"Ah, that is often the way with those of us
who create. Criticism by amateurs is like frost
on a spring sapling."

"Ummm, no doubt," Gerald said, wondering whether or not he wanted Belinda to be
painted by this rather extraordinary person
who, in an elliptical way, had just insulted
him. Still, his presence in the library would

serve a definite purpose. The sittings, which might take several hours, would assure him extra time with Felice without the need to invent elaborate excuses concerning his absence from the house. At that thought his still-smoldering resentment over the twin losses of freedom and love manifested itself and banished the distrust he had originally experienced upon meeting the strikingly handsome artist. He would be killing two birds with one stone, if one ought to use so malignant an aphorism.

He said, "When could you begin work on the portrait, Monsieur de Beaufort?"

"I am finishing a portrait at present. In a fortnight's time, I could begin work on the portrait of your lady. Would that be agreeable?"

"I expect it must be," Gerald said disappointedly, wishing that it were possible for the artist to begin at once.

"Very well, my lord, I am at your service, then."

Some five hours after his meeting with the artist, Gerald was further salving his conscience by escorting Belinda and Cornelia to Vauxhall Gardens. With them was the gallant he had invited for Lady Cornelia, Sir Fabian Gilchrist, a lively youth who evidently had a thorough knowledge of the famous pleasure gardens, one that encompassed the past as well as the present.

Notwithstanding the fact that he was there to escort Cornelia, Sir Fabian had attached himself to Belinda and was saying, as they approached the entrance, that he much regretted the fact that it was now possible to reach Vauxhall by coach rather than over the Thames in a boat, which might be accompanied by another boat in which musicians played them across the water. However, in those days there had been none of the fireworks that had just this year become a permanent part of the festivities. There had been many recent changes in the gardens, including the colonnade that stretched over the Grand Walk and that part of the area called the Grove.

Unfortunately for Sir Fabian's knowledgeable if extremely tiresome discourse, his listener's interest was suddenly distracted by the sight of a tall gentleman who appeared to be having words with a slender, graceful young woman who was staring up at him, her face turned ugly by anger. Then, with a stamp of one small foot, she whirled and disappeared amidst the crowds. Her escort made no effort to pursue her. Instead, he turned toward the entrance, and in that same moment Cornelia exclaimed, "But there is Lord—"

"Furneaux," Belinda finished excitedly.

"And," Sir Fabian laughed, "the little lady was Kitty O'Sullivan of the opera ballet."

"An opera dancer!" Cornelia exclaimed.

"The same." Sir Fabian continued to laugh. "And in a pet with her protector, it would seem."

"Fabian," Gerald admonished. "I hardly think that the ladies are interested in these suppositions."

"Oh, no, no, I do not think they would be," Sir Fabian said, flushing with embarrassment. "Beg pardon, ladies, beg pardon."

Unfortunately—or fortunately, depending on the thoughts coursing through the minds of that foursome—Lord Furneaux's gaze fell upon them. Rather than appearing discomfited, he hailed them and strode forward quickly to greet them, bowing over the outstretched hands of the ladies and subsequently exchanging warm greetings with Lord Courtenay and Sir Fabian. These over, he turned back to Belinda, "But I have not seen you since your wedding day, my dear," he said warmly. "I expect you have been on a journey?"

"We were," she acknowledged, thinking that he was even more handsome than he had appeared that day. "We were in Brighton, you know."

"Oh, yes, Brighton." He nodded. "I think that Lady Elizabeth did tell me you were going to Brighton. I hope you found it enjoyable?"

"Actually, we came home early," Belinda replied. "I caught a wretched cold and poor Gerald contracted it."

"I am sorry," he said. "But you must have recovered very quickly. You are looking very lovely tonight."

"I do thank you, my lord," she murmured, speaking over a pounding in her throat.

"And you, my dear"—Lord Furneaux turned toward Cornelia—"I understand that you have extended your stay in London."

She nodded. "Yes, Lady Elizabeth asked me

to remain for another month. Was that not kind of her?"

"I am very fond of Lady Elizabeth," he said, lowering his voice, "but I would imagine that the kindness was not entirely on her side."

"But I do enjoy her company," Cornelia assured him. "She knows so very much about gardening."

"Indeed? And would you be gifted with a green thumb too, my dear?"

"Indeed she is," Belinda said warmly. "She knows many of the Latin names for the plants and flowers. Aunt Elizabeth was truly amazed at her knowledge. In addition to that, she knows a great deal about herbs."

"Gracious, Belinda, you will have Lord Furneaux believing me a bluestocking!" Cornelia murmured.

"No," Belinda laughed. "I reserve that distinction for myself, or at least I have until recently."

"And what might that mean, my dear Belinda?" Lord Furneaux smiled down at her.

It was reprehensible of her, she knew, but Belinda was delighted to have garnered his attention again. After all, he was her particular friend and Cornelia little more than an acquaintance—and quite truthfully, when they had been chatting so companionably, there had been a moment when she had wished dearest Cornelia on the other side of the gardens or, better yet, safely with her Aunt Elizabeth in London! As soon as this notion crossed her mind, she was ashamed of herself, wishing that she had not deliberately interrupted the little conversation Cornelia had appeared to be enjoying so much. Then she remembered that he had asked her a question. "You know about my writing, of course."

"Of course," he assented immediately. "How would I not know, when I have read some of your earliest works."

"She has written two thrilling books!" Cornelia exclaimed. She added warmly, "I think that they are quite good enough to be published."

"Indeed? But, of course, I am not surprised, especially when I remember her essays and, I seem to recall, a short story about a horse, which proved most moving."

"Fancy your remembering that!" Belinda exclaimed.

He smiled at her. "But why would I not remember, my dear child? It was not half an aeon ago or even the better part of a century."

"You have read my wife's two books?" Gerald stepped to Belinda's side.

Lord Furneaux smiled down at Belinda. "No, I have not had that privilege, but I have read some of her other work. She has also penned some delightful poems."

"Are you a bluestocking, then?" Sir Fabian asked, goggling at Belinda.

"I beg you will give her the game without the name, please," Lord Furneaux protested. "She has considerable talent to writing, but one could never call her stockings blue."

"Anthony . . ." His lordship's given name

was being uttered in sweet bell-like tones from a short distance away.

Turning, Belinda saw the girl who had left his lordship in such a burst of anger, standing a few yards away, smiling shyly yet beguilingly in his direction.

"I think we had best see more of what the gardens have to offer us," Gerald said abruptly as he slipped a protective arm around his wife's waist.

"Yes, by all means," Sir Fabian exclaimed. "They have some capital dancing here . . . and the wicked waltz is a great favorite, I might add. I hope you will waltz with me, Lady Cornelia?"

"I will be delighted." She smiled. "And I do not believe it to be wicked."

"Indeed, it is not," Lord Furneaux agreed. "It is only those old tabbies at Almack's who insist that it is." He looked from Belinda to Cornelia. "I wish I might tread a measure with you ladies, but I think I must go to my little friend yonder. I see that she is in a better humor now, and I find that I am too." He bowed. "It was delightful meeting you . . . so unexpectedly. And may I hope that you will have a very pleasant evening."

"We hope the same for you." Belinda said.

As Lord Furneaux joined the girl, Sir Fabian said with a slight sneer. "I imagine she must cost him a pretty penny. I'd be damned if I would put up with her tantrums."

"She *is* very pretty," Cornelia murmured. "And so graceful. She moves as if she were dancing."

Hearing a slight catch in Cornelia's tones, Belinda was suddenly conscience-stricken, knowing that she had deliberately interrupted a conversation that her friend had been savoring. There was no doubt about it, she suddenly realized. For all that eighteen years stretched between them, Cornelia liked and might more than merely like his handsome lordship. Still, he was nineteen years older than she herself and she, too, more than liked him. In fact, she and Cornelia might very easily be rivals for his affection. She was conscious of a strong surge of jealousy. Then she swallowed a wry laugh. She was being utterly, utterly ridiculous! As a married woman, she could not be a rival to anyone unless she wished to create a horrid scandal!

Fortunately for her peace of mind, Belinda's melancholy thoughts were diverted by the sight of a glittering edifice half-hidden by the trees.

"Ah, yonder's the Rotunda!" Sir Fabian exclaimed. "It is lighted by no fewer than five thousand glass lamps."

"Five thousand, fancy!" Cornelia exclaimed, raising her voice so that she might be heard above the babble of voices and the sound of the orchestra, which was, Sir Fabian had said, ensconced in the second tier of the Rotunda.

"And," he yelled, "I've heard that old Hook is still there."

"Who is old Hook?" Gerald asked.

"The organist. Thirty-three years, he's been in the Gardens. And judging from what I have heard, he's like to be here another thirty-three."

"That would be James Hook," Cornelia said. "He writes songs, but they are not very good."

"No," Sir Fabian agreed. "He's a much better organist than he is a songwriter."

Belinda, moving from the circle of her husband's arm, edged a little nearer to the glittering edifice. The lights were arranged in patterns, and also they outlined the fanciful dome. It was, she thought, not only a brilliant spectacle, but a dizzying one as well, sending a flurry of red and green spots dancing before her eyes. She tried to blink them away, and in that same moment a hand closed on her arm and a rough voice demanded jocularly, "And who are you, my pretty maid?"

Looking up in amazement, she discovered a large and extremely unprepossessing man looming over her. He was clad in cheap but flamboyant garments and he had small mean eyes set in a plump face. His mouth, full and loose-lipped, was stretched into a grin which, for some reason she could not define, gave Belinda the shudders. A quick, frightened glance about her showed her that she had become separated from Gerald and the others. She said icily, "That is no concern of yours, sir. And I will thank you to release my arm."

He laughed loudly. "By God, that is a new approach, that is. A doxy wi' airs'n graces. But, by God, yet a pretty creature'n I'll be glad to pay yer price, lovey."

"You will please let me go!" Belinda tried to pull away.

Her captor's grip turned hurtful. "No, you don't, my lovely. Yer comin' wi' me. Us'll 'ave a merry time o' it, see if we don't."

"Gerald . . . Gerald . . ." Belinda screamed, looking in vain for a sight of her husband and her friends.

"Stow yer gab," her captor growled. "I can . . ." Whatever else he might have said died on his lips as he was suddenly confronted by an angry Gerald.

"Release my wife, damn you," he ordered.

"Yer . . . wife?" the other snarled. "A likely tale'n 'er walkin' down the path as bold as you please. I'll 'ave yer worship know that my money's as good as yours when it comes to pleasurin' the likes o'er." He started to pull a terrified and struggling Belinda away, but then went staggering back as Gerald struck him a heavy blow to the chin.

Taking advantage of her captor's suddenly loosened hold, Belinda dashed to Gerald's side as another man, who had stopped to witness the confrontation, cried admiringly, "By God, that were a facer, for sure."

" 'Ave at 'im," shrilled a lad. "Let's 'ave us a mill!"

"A mill! A mill!" chorused several other interested spectators, one of them adding in admiring tones, "I'll lay my blunt on the swell."

Fortunately, the big man, a hand to his assaulted chin, appeared to have lost his enthusiasm for a confrontation with his assailant. "All ri' . . . all ri'," he growled. " 'Ave the doxy'n be damned to the both o' ye." He lurched away quickly and was lost in the crowds, much to the disappointment of his expectant audience.

"Come away, my dear," Gerald urged, slipping his arm around Belinda's waist.

"Oh, G-Gerald." Belinda, clinging to him, shuddered. "Oh, I . . . I was so frightened."

He stared down at her, half-annoyed, half-pitying. "You should not have wandered away from me, my dear. Wherever did you go?"

"I did not go anywhere," she said defensively. "At least, I was not aware of it. I . . . I was just walking along looking at all the pretty colored lights and . . . and then, suddenly, he was there . . ." She shuddered.

His arm tightened. "Shhh, my dearest," he said gently. "It is all over now and you are safe. But you must stay close by me from now on. Indeed, I will make sure that you do." He reached down to clasp her hand as he led her through the crowds to where an anxious Cornelia stood with Sir Fabian. "I have found her!" he said triumphantly.

"Oh, Belinda! Wherever did you go? We were so very concerned," Cornelia said.

"I did not realize that I was falling behind," Belinda explained, "not until that . . . that person accosted me."

"You were accosted?" Cornelia asked.

"She was," Gerald said grimly, "and by a rogue who, I hope, will think twice before he attempts it again."

"You did give him a . . . a facer, is it?" Belinda smiled up at Gerald.

"A facer, eh? I wish I'd been there to see it," Sir Fabian said regretfully. "Gerald, here, has always been handy with his fives."

"I should have liked to have given that lout a great deal more than a mere facer." Gerald frowned. "The way he was looking at Belinda . . ."

Belinda suddenly giggled. "He took me for a doxy."

"He did not!" Cornelia said in horror.

"Oh, yes, he did. He said he'd be glad to pay my price."

"Damn him! If I had known that, I would have sent his teeth down his damned throat," Gerald said furiously.

"Oh, listen," Cornelia said suddenly. "They are playing a waltz. Do let us go and watch the dancers!"

"I think that it is time and past that we left," Gerald said.

"Oh, please, no," Belinda protested. "I would love to see them waltz." She looked up at her husband. "I promise I will not wander off again, Gerald."

"Do you?" he asked teasingly. "I promise that I will not let you wander off again, because I mean to keep both an eye and a hand on you . . . while we watch the dancers."

In a few moments they had arrived at a platform in the Rotunda, where a great many smiling couples were whirling around the floor to the sprightly music from an orchestra located on a level several feet above them.

"Oh, look," Belinda exclaimed in surprise. "They are holding each other so very closely."

"That is why it is called the 'wicked' waltz," Cornelia murmured.

"My dear . . ." Gerald's arm tightened about Belinda's waist. "Would you like to join them?"

She regarded him eagerly and nervously at the same time. "I . . . I have never danced the waltz in a public place."

He raised his eyebrows. "I hope you will not tell me that you, too, count yourself among those who still disapprove of it."

"Oh, no, I am telling you that I have danced it only with my younger sister, Pansy, at home. Our teacher refused to instruct us in it. She did not approve of it, certainly. In fact, now that I think of it, she, too, said it was wicked."

"I assure you that it will not be wicked when you are treading a measure with me," he laughed. "Come, my dear."

Since he was inexorably leading her toward the dancers as he was talking, Belinda had no choice but to obey, and with a surge of excitement she discovered within herself a strong desire to dance with Gerald. She was feeling . . . She was not quite able to interpret her feelings at this particular moment, save that she had a strong desire to be with him. She only hoped that she would be able to follow him.

Gerald proved to be an excellent dancer and Belinda's secret lessons stood her in good stead as they whirled about the floor. In fact, she was extremely sorry when the music ended, and greatly pleased when another waltz was immediately announced, especially since Gerald insisted that they remain on the floor.

"You are uncommonly graceful, my dear," he told her.

"I thank you." She smiled up at him. "I do enjoy waltzing with you."

"And I am delighted to waltz with you, my dear." He drew her into his arms again as the music began once more. "It is a great pity that it is not allowed at Almack's."

"I expect that the hostesses believe that it is too daring," Belinda murmured.

"Actually, I suppose that it might be so considered." He nodded, and was silent as he executed a complicated turn. Then he continued, "But for those of us who are married, it certainly ought to be permitted."

Belinda cast a mischievous look about her and observed laughingly, "Do you imagine that all the dancers here are married?"

He laughed too. "I am quite sure they are not. We are probably the only respectable people present."

"Oh, dear . . . oh, dear, that does sound so dreadfully dull," she said.

Gerald raised his eyebrows. "My dearest Belinda, am I to infer that you find respectability . . . dull?" he asked.

"Perhaps I find it so . . . tonight." She gave him a provocative smile.

He whirled her around again. "And so do I . . . tonight," he admitted as he drew her closer to him. "Do you know, my dear, that there are little flames in your eyes?"

She giggled. "It is far from kind of you to tell me that I have red eyes, sir."

"On the contrary," he murmured. "I am

telling you that you have beguiling eyes, my dearest. I am saying that they are also magnetic, drawing me down, down, down into their emerald depths. Mermaids luring hapless sailors to their deaths might possess such eyes, and if I were to drown in them, I would die with pleasure."

It was on the tip of her tongue to scold him, telling him that he was talking nonsense, and then laugh . . . but neither the words nor the laughter would emerge. On the contrary, Belinda was finding that she did not want to talk at all. She only wanted to feel Gerald's strong arms around her as they moved together in time to the music, the enchanting music. And the waltz was wicked, she decided, for its cadences seemed to be invading her, causing her to wish that it would never, never end, and that wish was, in turn, engendered by the heady excitement of her husband's nearness.

Of course, it did end, and since they were both breathless, Belinda and Gerald left the floor and joined Cornelia and Sir Fabian, who had left the platform much earlier, neither looking as if they had enjoyed themselves half as much as she had—or rather, she and her husband.

Time seemed to accelerate, once the dance had ended. After they had strolled down an illuminated lane, admiring the colored lights attached to the trees and plants, and had stopped to listen as a prima donna from the opera sang selections from *The Maid of the Mill* and *The Beggar's Opera*, they partook of refreshments at a booth. These included heady drafts of champagne, which made Belinda feel so dizzy that she nearly fell and probably would have had not Gerald's arm been around her. He smiled down at her. "I think we must leave, my dear, don't you?"

"Oh, yes," Cornelia, overhearing him, agreed.

"Mus' leave, mus' definitely leave," was Sir Fabian's slurred response.

"Mus'," Belinda echoed. "Oh!" she exclaimed as Gerald suddenly scooped her up in his arms and carried her all the way out of the gardens and into the waiting coach. Still, tipsy or not, it had been a lovely evening and she was sorry that it was at an end, which she told Gerald as he insisted on carrying her up the stairs to the second floor of their house.

Just as they reached that landing, the clock struck the hour, a single crystalline note, not followed by another chime.

"One," Belinda said, adding confusedly, "Does not anything follow one?"

"Not when one is all there is," Gerald said reasonably.

"Shouldn't two follow one?" she asked.

"Two will follow one, my darling, when the hands of the clock indicate that it is two," he explained, and laughed. "I fear that you are still tipsy, my love."

"No, I am not, not anymore. At least, I do not believe I am. Ohhhhh." She smiled up at him. "It was so lovely, so very lovely dancing with you."

"I am in complete agreement—it was very lovely for me as well."

"I did not want the dance to end, not ever."

"The dance has ended, but this night has not ended, my love," he said softly.

"But . . . but if it is one, it is morning."

"A beautiful, dark morning, though. The darkness is all about us and the moon still shines and the stars are still out and we are together—and, my love, I have been a fool."

"No, never a fool, Gerald," she protested.

"Then, foolish, surely."

"I . . . I do not understand you," she murmured confusedly.

"I certainly do not understand myself, my beautiful." He kissed her.

It was a very different kiss than any she had ever received before and it was certainly longer and it filled her with a strange excitement, so that when finally he raised his head, she wound her arms around his neck, whispering, "Again . . . please, again."

"Soon," he murmured.

Belinda was aware of being carried into a chamber that was dimly lit, as her chamber was before Mary blew out the candles, but though she glanced about her, looking for her abigail, she did not see her. Then she was placed on a bed and her garments were being removed, and every so often a kiss fell upon her—on her shoulder, the little hollow at the base of her throat—and then she was lying on softness and held against warmth and hearing her name rapturously pronounced by her husband. Then a rising confusion was replaced by feelings she had never experienced before, and concurrent with these was a mounting excitement, a momentary pain, and a strange floating sensation, and later, much later, a marvelous closeness during which she fell deeply asleep wrapped in her husband's arms.

4

"But I have not seen or heard from you in nearly three weeks!" Cornelia said as, once again, she and Belinda took their seats at a table in the tearoom at Hardy, Howell & Company, Ltd. "And," she added before Belinda could respond, "is that not another new gown?"

Belinda nodded. "Yes. I found the material in Oxford, if you can imagine. It is a shade of green I have never seen before."

"Yes, it is deeper and darker and very becoming. And so you were in Oxford?"

"Yes, Gerald wanted to show me through the university. He attended Oxford, you know. We also visited Stratford-upon-Avon. He said that as a writer, I must see where Shakespeare was buried."

"Evidently you enjoyed yourself," Cornelia observed.

"Oh, we certainly did. We stayed at the most charming inn and . . ." Belinda broke off and then said softly, meaningfully. "We are so very . . . very happy, Cornelia."

"But I know that, my dear," Cornelia responded softly.

Belinda's eyes widened in surprise. "However did you guess?"

"How could I not guess, Belinda? You are looking so beautiful, and more than that, you seem contented."

"Yes, yes, yes, I am. Oh, I am." Belinda lowered her voice. "I do wish you might be married, my dearest Cornelia. Is there no one for whom you believe you might care?"

Cornelia smiled deprecatingly. "I am afraid not. My mother and my aunt, too, will be extremely disappointed. They had hoped that this Season with Lady Elizabeth would produce a husband. They will have to pin their hopes on Caroline. She is very pretty. She is also much more lively than I—and, of course, she is two years younger."

"Two years?" Belinda questioned in surprise. "How is that possible? Caroline is eighteen and you—"

"Caroline has just had her eighteenth birthday," Cornelia interrupted. "As for myself, I am twenty. I reached that aged condition last week."

"Oh! Oh, dear!" Belinda cried. "Your birthday, and I forgot! It was last Tuesday."

"Tuesday, yes, and so when I go home in mid-September, I will resign myself to being a prop to Mama . . . or to my aunt," Cornelia said wryly.

"Oh, Cornelia," Belinda protested. "Twenty is not *old*, certainly. And furthermore, there

have been many young men who have been
attracted to you."

"I have not been attracted to them—and
since Mama and my aunt have assured me
that I may follow the dictates of my heart—"

"Is there no one you have liked?" Belinda
interrupted.

"No one who could marry me," Cornelia
responded with a little sigh.

"Then there *is* someone," Belinda pursued
excitedly. "Do I know him?" The moment those
ill-considered words left her lips, she longed
to recall them. In her mind's eye she had an
image of Lord Furneaux on the night they
had met him at Vauxhall Gardens. On that
night, he had managed to destroy two illu-
sions for Cornelia, she was quite sure—these
being that he was still devastated over the
death of his wife and the other that he might
eventually be persuaded to marry again. Cornelia was no fool. She would have understood that Lord Furneaux was not hankering
for any changes in his present mode of exis-
tence.

"There is no one for whom I care," Cornelia
said firmly. "Mama and Aunt will understand
my position. Mama married for love and my
aunt did not marry because she loved someone she could not marry."

"Yes, but if one does not have a choice, love
can come later," Belinda said softly.

"As it obviously has to you, my dear." Cornelia smiled at her. "Really, Belinda, I could
not be more pleased that Gerald has finally
come to his senses. I had a feeling he would

when I saw you dancing together that night at Vauxhall Gardens. Indeed, I would not be surprised to discover that he loved you from the first and did not know his own mind."

"I think you are wrong about that," Belinda responded thoughtfully. "It . . . it was when we came home that night . . . that he became so . . . so very fond."

"You are suggesting that he was hit by a bolt from the blue—one of Cupid's arrows? I am sure that you are mistaken, my dear."

"You prefer to believe that because you are my friend," Belinda said, "but no matter, we are very happy."

"And you are to have your portrait painted."

Belinda nodded. "I met the artist yesterday. He is French and very handsome. He is also taller than most of the Frenchmen I have met. I expect that is because he comes from Normandy. I understand that the Norman French are taller than those born in the south. His name is Chrétien de Beaufort. I do not think Gerald likes him . . . in fact, if I had not interceded, I think he might have dismissed him."

"Oh? Why would he not like him?"

"I expect it was mainly because he insisted that Gerald not come to the sittings. He does not permit 'outsiders' to disrupt his concentration. He must establish a rapport with his subject and he has said that he finds this impossible when there is another person in the room. Gerald, of course, believes his attitude high-handed and, of course, it is. Still, I have a feeling that it is a part of his nature. I think he might have been born to command, as it were. He has an air, certainly. I suppose he is a member of the French aristocracy."

Cornelia laughed. "Possibly he is, my dear, but I have heard it said that if every Frenchman who declares that he was turned out of his château is to be believed, then France would not have suffered a revolution, for the whole country would have given over to the aristocracy."

"Yes, I have heard that myself." Belinda nodded. "But if you were to meet Monsieur de Beaufort, you would understand what I mean. He is certainly not a man of the people."

"I hope that he is a good artist," Cornelia said dryly.

"Oh, I am sure he is," Belinda responded enthusiastically. "Gerald took me to the Royal Academy and we saw one of his paintings. It is entitled *The Virgin at the Well*. It was quite wonderful, and I am glad that he is going to paint me. I am sure that Gerald will be pleased with the results."

"I am sure he will, my dear. He seems to be entirely in accord with you."

"You have really not seen us together of late," Belinda pointed out.

"I saw you at Vauxhall Gardens, my dear."

"But that was before . . ." Belinda paused and looked down suddenly, her cheeks very red.

"I watched you dancing together," Cornelia pursued. "If ever a man looked blissful—"

"Do you really think he did?" Belinda interrupted.

"I am sure that you do not require my corroboration now."

"Well, perhaps not, but at first . . . But I do not want to think about that." Belinda shivered slightly.

"And nor should you," Cornelia said pointedly. "That is all in the past."

"But what more can I tell you about Monsieur de Beaufort, Gerald, dearest?" Felice asked, smiling up into his frowning face. "I do not deny that he is autocratic. He likes quiet when he works, and he feels that if outsiders are present, the rapport between subject and artist is disturbed, if not destroyed."

"I expect that I understand his cavils," Gerald admitted reluctantly. "But still, for her husband, I think an exception could certainly be made."

Felice studied his frowning face a moment before saying with more than a hint of reproach in her tones, "I had the impression that one of the reasons we decided that your wife must be painted was for our own convenience. You had been complaining because it was difficult to find excuses to leave the house for such long periods of time. And, indeed, it must have been very difficult for you of late, for I have not seen you for at least three weeks."

"I told you that we went out of town. It was necessary to give her at least a semblance of a wedding journey . . . the poor child was miserable in Brighton."

"And she was not miserable in Oxford and

beyond?" Felice asked with just the suggestion of an edge to her tone.

He was briefly silent as he pondered an answer. She was right, of course, regarding the portrait. It had been a ploy, and how could he now explain to her about the aftermath of that reluctant visit to Vauxhall Gardens? He could scarcely tell her that it had, in effect, brought him a happiness which exceeded anything he had ever known—a happiness that had finally taught him the true meaning of love. It had also made him wish that he had never met Felice, never agreed to that ugly little stratagem that had brought Chrétien, the artist, into his life—Chrétien, whom he did not like and whom he instinctively distrusted, and whose presence might be responsible for the black horse that had galloped through his dreams last night.

He said uncomfortably, "There are still problems," and hoped that Felice could not read the anger in his eyes. He was angry with himself, very angry indeed as he contemplated the scheme he had evolved with Felice—or rather the scheme she had suggested—from the span of a fortnight. A mere fourteen days had passed, but these two weeks had been the most important pair of weeks of his entire life! It was then that he had fallen deeply, irrevocably in love with his wife—to the point that he wanted nothing more to do with Felice. He had found it extraordinarily difficult even to embrace her when he came in—and now he most desperately longed to leave and never show his face in her studio again!

Unfortunately, he could not cut her off so summarily, even though he was well aware that many other young men of his own personal acquaintance had dismissed their mistresses very easily. Of course, such partings were invariably costly, and he would have been more than willing to settle a large sum of money on Felice, but though he had, on occasion, and only over her vociferous protests, given her money, he had always assured her that he loved her and he had always received similar assurances in return. He wished strongly that he could believe them false, but that was impossible. Felice did love him, and when he had begun his relationship with her, he had not known the true meaning of love. Indeed, where could he have found it? Not in Spain, surely, among the wanton camp followers or the equally wanton women of the towns, who went with anyone who could pay them.

As it must come to many, true love had stolen upon him unawares, and it was only in the last fortnight that he had entered into the realms of ecstasy, and in so entering, had finally learned the difference between lust and love.

Beside his radiant bride, Felice seemed suddenly older and perhaps a little weary. By her own admission, she had known other men. She had assured him, of course, that they meant nothing to her. Still, assurances were easy to mouth, especially when the listening lover was as inexperienced as himself! He wished he were still inexperienced—he wished he might have shared that delightful discovery of passion with Belinda. A vision of her, lying asleep beside him this morning with the rosy glow of dawn on her upturned face, made him wish that he were away from here and with her at this very moment.

"You are so silent, Gerald," Felice said. "You seem not in a good mood."

He resented her intrusion into his thoughts, airy bubbles of thoughts, rainbow-hued. It was with reluctance that he provided a smile and an explanation. "I have much on my mind, my dear. I have discovered that being married has its own set of problems."

"I am sure that it must," she said sympathetically, "but I am in hopes that those problems will be solved by Chrétien."

He stiffened. "What would you be meaning by that, my dear?" he demanded edgily.

Felice regarded him with blank surprise. "While he is painting her picture, you will be with me, will you not?"

"I . . . hope that I will be able to find the time," he said uncomfortably.

Her eyes widened. "The time . . . But he will not be able to paint the portrait in a day, you know."

"I know that, of course," he replied, striving to keep a strain of impatience out of his tone. "But I must also have discussions with my man of business regarding properties that I own independently of my father. It may be that I will wish to make certain improvements in one of my houses or possibly build a new one. You must understand that my life has undergone certain changes."

"I begin to understand many things." Felice moved closer to him. "I begin to understand that perhaps you are not as happy to see me as I am to see you."

Her guess came so near the truth that he found himself denying it vociferously and ending a rather long and involved explanation with the words, "Why would I not be happy to see you? Nothing has changed between us, Felice."

She gave him a long, penetrating look before saying, coolly, "She must be very lovely, your bride."

"I have told you, Felice . . ." Pity and shame brought his arm around her. However, he drew back quickly as she began to loosen his cravat. "You will undo the hard work of my valet," he said half in annoyance.

She laughed, but took her hands away from his cravat, sliding them under his shirt and beginning to caress him, teasing little touches that had once thrilled him but now spoke to him of practice rather than spontaneity. An image of Belinda's shy, tentative responses made him ache with longing for her. He said abruptly, "As I have told you, Felice, I must go. On this day, my time is not entirely my own."

Her hands fell to her sides. She raised reproachful eyes and let them linger on his face. "I thought it might happen," she sighed.

"I do not understand you. What do you mean?" he asked uncomfortably.

"I think you know without my saying, Gerald. You have fallen in love with her and out of love with me."

"No," he said uncomfortably. "I have appointments today, but I do not have them every day, and I will be back, I assure you."

"When?" she demanded unwisely, knowing that to question him was the height of foolishness, but still this was Gerald, Gerald, her lover, who had railed against the marriage so summarily thrust upon him. Could this inexperienced girl have stolen him from her so soon? Perhaps. Yet, not for long, Felice thought. Undoubtedly she was no more than a passing fancy, and once he had his fill of innocence and ignorance, he would return. Then she would have her revenge, she would make him beg for her favors on his knees! However, until that glorious moment, she must be clever. He had not answered her question yet, and she said, "But it does not matter when you return, Gerald, my love. Tonight, tomorrow, a week hence, or a fortnight." The words "a month, two months, six . . ." trembled on her tongue and were swallowed because she was not quite brave enough to voice them.

"It will not be a fortnight, Felice," he felt himself obliged to assure her. He bent to kiss her lightly on the lips. He was pleased that she had not wound her arms around his neck and strained herself against him, as was usually her wont. He was also pleased that she had not asked him when she would see him again—at least, she had not specifically mentioned a time. He had a strong feeling that she understood what he was trying to tell her, and because of that, he kissed her again and with more fervor than before. Then he gladly took his leave.

Shortly after her arrival, Belinda had decided that the library was her favorite of all the beautiful chambers in Gerald's London mansion. She had always been partial to white marble fireplaces flanked by caryatids carved in black marble and holding up mahogany mantelshelves. She also loved the tall shelves of books that rose to the ceiling on opposite sides of the room, and the long windows that rose on either side of the fireplace. She was particularly fond of the comfortable furnishings and she took great delight in the oil painting that showed Gerald in his scarlet uniform riding a mettlesome black horse through a green field under a lowering cloud-filled sky.

Her pleasure in that scene was not in the least dimmed by Gerald's laughing confidence that the steed and its rider had been painted at different times, and nor was she disappointed to learn that the stormy sky was a figment of the artist's imagination. The effect was what counted, and she thought it both striking and beautiful.

Consequently, she had been quite annoyed when Chrétien de Beaufort had said with laughter reflected in his dark eyes, "A popular pose. The artist tries to make up in detail what he lacks in imagination. See how perfectly the stirrups are reproduced, and the uniform is another miracle. It lacks only the chasing on the buttons."

"I think it is magnificent," Belinda had retorted defiantly.

"But, of course, you would think that it is magnificent, my dear," he had said so loftily that she had longed to dismiss him on the spot. However, on this, his second visit, he was making preliminary sketches on a large pad of paper with a stick of charcoal. He did not seem pleased with what he was doing, for he had muttered various words under his breath and had angrily crumpled three sheets of paper. Finally he looked up, and glaring at her accusingly rasped, "Why do you elude me?"

Belinda looked at him with a surprise tinged by anger. "I have not moved," she said hotly.

"Did I say you had?" he demanded.

Her surprise increased. "But you have just told me that I eluded you," she pointed out.

"*You* elude me, my dear Lady Courtenay, and when I say 'you,' I speak not of your charming self, but of essences. Generally, when I paint a woman, I know exactly what I wish from her and it does not take long to decide on the effect I wish, but you . . . you, milady, defy me."

"That is not my intention, Monsieur de Beaufort. Tell me what you wish me to do and I will do it," she said.

His eyes widened and then he laughed. "So provocative and so innocent," he mused. He brought his hands together in a resounding

clap. "*Oui, oui, oui, c'est magnifique!* It is
the effect I wish to achieve. I am thinking of
a young Lucretia, perhaps, or even of a
Paulina—but before either had awakened."

"Lucretia . . . Paulina?" Belinda questioned
confusedly.

"And," he said in some surprise, "they are
both B's."

"Bees?" Belinda's confusion had increased.

He laughed again. "The one B was a Borgia
and the other was a Bonaparte—*is* a Bonaparte and has yet another B to her name,
Borghese, which should soften the Bonaparte,
should it not? I am speaking, of course, of
Paulina Bonaparte, the lovely little sister of
our corporal-who-would-be-Caesar. Ah, such
a charming upstart. She has, I understand,
done quite a bit of conquering in her own
right. Yet, at the same time, she is oddly
innocent. Do you know, it is said that when
our little Paulina was criticized for posing for
Canova's recumbent and gloriously nude
statue of her perfect self, she was surprised
and said, "But there was a fire in the room."

"Oh!" Belinda could not suppress a giggle.

"Ah, I like that expression. I see that I will
have to paint a smiling portrait. I have never
cared for them, but your smile must be im-
mortalized. I hope that your husband will
agree with me."

She was very glad that he had mentioned
her husband, for it had occurred to her that
he was becoming far too familiar. She said, "I
do not mind smiling . . . but I would not pose
as Paulina posed, Monsieur de Beaufort."

"And I would not require that pose from you, even were your husband to acquiesce, which I am quite sure he would not."

"I am equally sure of that, Monsieur de Beaufort," she said with just a touch of hauteur.

He seemed unaware of the coolness that had entered her tone. He said merely, "I think that I know how I will paint you . . ." He regarded her in silence for a moment and nodded. "Yes, I do know. I must leave now, but tomorrow, if we may start work at the same hour as today . . . Is that possible?"

"Yes, I can arrange my time around it." Belinda nodded.

"I am glad. And also, I would appreciate your husband's presence, so that I might give him my notions concerning the portrait."

"I will give him your message, Monsieur de Beaufort," Belinda said.

"Then I will wish you a good afternoon, milady."

She had not expected that he would stride to her side and bear her hand to his lips, but the kiss he pressed on it was so fleeting that before she could utter the cool little set-down that had sprung to her mind, if not to her tongue, he had bowed and swiftly taken his leave.

Within that same hour, Chrétien returned to the Village of Chelsea. His studio was not far from that of Felice, and once he had disposed of the materials he had brought with him, he hurried out and covered the distance between their two streets in minutes.

In another few minutes he was knocking peremptorily upon Felice's door. After several minutes that portal was opened cautiously, and as he had anticipated, Chrétien found the traces of tears on Felice's cheeks. There was also a reddening of her eyes. Without preamble, he shrugged and said, "But it is very unfortunate, of course, my Felice, but she is adorable."

"Go away!" Felice cried angrily, and tried to slam the door in his face, but he pushed it back, letting it crash against the wall.

"We must have a conversation, my dear," he said determinedly.

"I do not wish to speak to you," she protested.

He closed the door quietly and stood with his back against it. "I am sure you do not," he said coolly. "Just as I am equally sure that you are aware that I have come from a second discussion with the beautiful little bride of your lover."

"Of course I know it," she snapped. "Must you continue to torture me? Have I not suffered enough? Go, go, go," she ordered shrilly. "I do not wish to speak to you. I have suffered enough already. There is nothing more to say."

"Do you not know that repetition only weakens a statement, my dear?" He shook his head. "It seems to me, my dearest Felice, that you have made the monumental error of falling in love with your lover. Lovers should be victims, not victors in this game of love, or, to call it by its rightful name, prurience. Did you let him see your tears?"

She shook her head. "No, of course not. But, Chrétien, I beg of you, go. I am not in the mood to speak to you . . . or anyone."

He remained where he was, his back against the door. He said calmly, "If you force me to leave, you will not hear what I have to tell you, and that would be a mistake, because I might not be so minded upon another day. However, my dearest Felice, since you did me the great favor of procuring this commission for me, a far greater favor than you are, perhaps, aware, I feel that I should reward you in some way."

"I . . . I do not need money," she snapped.

"But I have no intention of giving you money. In my present condition, I must garner every sou or rather ha'pence that comes my way. Still, I can express my gratitude in ways that have nothing to do with the exchange of coins and which might prove equally helpful to us both."

There was something in his tone that caused Felice to blink back her tears and eye him speculatively. "How might these ways prove helpful?" she asked.

He smiled. "Ah, that is better." He moved away from the door, and crossing to her sofa, stretched out upon it and smiled up at her. "I have great affection for you, Felice. I do not like to see you weep, especially over this English puppy."

Felice followed him to the sofa and sat down

on the far end of it. "Tell me about the bride," she commanded abruptly.

"She is beautiful, she is adorable, she is in love, and quite naturally, her husband has discovered that he is in love with her."

Tears appeared in Felice's eyes again. "Is this the help you offer . . . to break my heart?" she questioned with a sob.

"I beg you will not weep, my dear. I have come to tell you that we must form a . . . partnership."

"I do not under—"

"And you never will understand if you do not stop interrupting me," he said testily. "I can help you, Felice, but only if you will be quiet while I outline my plan. I do not wish to be treated to more of your tantrums or your sobs. Neither of these will bring your lover back to your bed. It requires a plan. Now, do I outline it to you or do I leave?"

"No . . . I would like to hear it."

"Good, very good, my love." He sat up, and coming to where she sat, drew her into his embrace and kissed her lingeringly.

She did not attempt to push him away. As usual, Chrétien's kisses warmed her. Long ago she had relinquished the hope that they signified anything more. History was full of change, and it might be possible that one day he would regain his estates, his titles, and marry a woman of his choice and of his class. Certainly she would not be that choice— she, the bastard offspring of a nobleman and a scene painter.

Chrétien kissed her again and then again.

Finally he pulled back from her, saying, "You are a sweet armful, Felice. Your lover will come back once he has had his fill of innocence, but he needs a push. Let us give it to him."

"A . . . push?" She regarded him quizzically. "I do not understand you."

"A push out of her marriage bed, my beautiful. She is in the throes of first love. It would be a pity to disillusion her, but were she to be disillusioned, I, for one, would not find it a tragedy."

"Ah . . ." Felice gave him a long look. "You are attracted to her yourself," she accused.

He smiled at her. "But of course, my dear. I am more than merely attracted to her. She is in my blood . . . I must possess her. I am quite madly in love with her."

"Oh, Chrétien!" Felice found that she could actually giggle. "You are completely incorrigible. You fall *madly* in love with every female you paint. And when you have had them, you discard them, *zut*! This regrettable habit has already lost you two very profitable commissions, to my certain knowledge, and on one occasion, if you will remember, it very nearly lost you your right arm!"

"But of course I remember, my dearest love." He gave her a fond smile. "And I might very well have lost it, were it not for your tender nursing. That is another reason why you possess my eternal gratitude and my desire to help you win back your rather uninteresting young lover."

"He . . . he is not uninteresting," she said

with the suggestion of a sob. "Of all the English whom I have known, he . . . He is not uninteresting," she concluded lamely.

He frowned. "Ah, that is not what I wish to hear, my love. You are suggesting, in effect, that I will have myself a formidable rival?"

"If you are determined on trying to possess his bride, yes." Felice gave him a half-laughing, half-reproachful look. "Why, why, why are you attracted to all your female sitters, my dearest Chrétien? One of these days it will catapult you into real danger."

"I was not attracted to Lady Cavendish." He grinned.

"Only because she was practically in her dotage when . . . was it her son-in-law who commissioned the portrait?" Felice laughed.

"I was not attracted to Marie Durand, who was my Virgin at the Well," he responded defensively. "And certainly you will not attempt to deny that she was young and very, very beautiful."

"Ah, no!" Felice rolled her eyes. "I will not deny it, and you, my own, will not say that you remained completely impervious to her charms. You are speaking to me, Felice. The only reason you did not make an attempt to have your wicked way with her was that her father, your very good friend and fellow artist, Jacques Durand, would have cut out your heart with his palette knife!"

"Very possibly," he admitted with a laugh. "However, we digress, my dearest. For now, let us concentrate on the adorable Belinda and also on your erstwhile lover, who ought to be chastised if only for his lack of gratitude in winning a love that is never given lightly. I am not speaking of his bride, my Felice."

"What can you do?" she asked dubiously.

"I have an idea. Do you remember that miniature that you gave me long ago, a charming and accurate self-portrait?"

"Yes, I remember. Do you still have it, then?" She looked at him with some surprise.

"But of course I still have it," he responded with a surprise that matched her own. "It is not something I would want to lose—ever. However, I am about to endanger it—in a good cause, I assure you. And I wish only to know that if I do: will you paint me another? It is a possession that I esteem most highly."

"Oh, Chrétien, Chrétien," she sighed. "Why do you love to tease me?"

"My dear, I am not teasing you," he said seriously. "But I must have your promise that you will paint me another—before I outline my plan."

"You will not tell me that you have already a plan, Chrétien!" Felice cried.

"I have already a plan, yes, my love, but first—your promise." He looked at her quite seriously.

"I will paint you another, of course, but now you must tell me what you intend!"

"I will, of course, my adorable Felice," he said with a smile.

5

Shortly after the clock on the mantelpiece in Gerald's chamber struck the hour of seven, Gerald slipped out of bed and stood staring down at his wife. She opened her eyes and smiled up at him adoringly. "You are up," she said unnecessarily.

"I have much to do today," he explained. He added, "And must I relinquish you to Monsieur de Beaufort again this morning?"

"You must." She nodded. "But I expect there will not be many more sittings. He is progressing rapidly."

"I wish I might see this masterpiece," he said a trifle resentfully.

"Soon," she assured him.

"I would like to know the reason for this secrecy." He frowned. "Why should I not view a painting in progress?"

"Because you agreed you would not," she said reasonably.

"I should not have agreed," he growled. "I should not have given in to his artistic quirks."

"But you did." She smiled.

"I have half a mind . . ." he threatened.

"No, Gerald!" she protested.

"I doubt that he would know the difference."

"He would know . . . he folds the cloth over it in a particular way, a way you could never duplicate."

"Oh, God." He rolled his eyes. "I hope, my love, that . . ." He sat down on the edge of the bed.

"That what?"

"That he does justice to your hair—though I doubt that he will. It is the color of sunlight on plums."

She giggled, and catching one of his hands, pretended to bite his finger. "You are saying that I have purple hair?"

"No, but 'red' seems far too mundane a term. . . . In common with Joseph's coat, it is many colors." He brought a shining strand to his lips. Then, stretching out beside her, he put his arms around her.

She lifted her face for a passionate kiss that lasted a gratifyingly long time, and murmured, "Oh, Gerald, I am so very happy."

"As I am, my own." He reluctantly released her. "But . . ."

"But?" she murmured.

"What were you saying to Furneaux last night? It seemed to me that you talked to him for quite a while!"

"I will tell you," Belinda said, "if you will tell me why *you* never stopped talking to that fair-haired lady who sat next to you at dinner. I did not catch her name when we were introduced."

"Her name is Lady Margaret Sewell, and let it be said that she never stopped talking to me." He gave her a long look. "You seem on excellent terms with Lord Furneaux."

She gave him a provocative look and said, "Of course I am on excellent terms with him. I always have been, for years and years and years."

"Indeed?" Gerald moved away from her and propped his head on his hand, staring down at her. "He is a little old for you to have known for years and years and years."

"He never seems old, not to me." Belinda giggled. "He is a dear friend of my brother James. They attended Cambridge together—and sometimes he came home with James. His parents died young and he enjoyed being with our family over the holidays."

"Did he stay with you after he left the university?"

"Oh, yes, before his marriage. He was twenty-five when he married."

Gerald loosed a breath. "You must have been a mere child."

"Very mere indeed," she admitted.

"No, I will not believe that." He dropped a kiss on her cheek. "No one could ever call you 'very mere.' "

"You are funning me," she accused.

"Perhaps," he admitted. He kissed her and pulled her into his arms again.

"Oh, Gerald," she said anxiously. "It is time we were astir."

"Who has ordered that we must be?" he demanded.

"It is half-past seven now."

"Do you have any strong objections to remaining with your adoring husband a little longer?"

"It was you who said you had much to do today," she reminded him.

"Do you have any strong objections to remaining with me a little while longer?"

"Well . . ."

"Well?" He slipped his hands under the covers and began to caress her.

She gazed up at him, her face suffused with blushes. Then, pressing herself against him, she said in a small voice, "No, my Gerald, I do not."

"Oh, my angel," he murmured ecstatically.

It was ten minutes past the hour of eleven when Gerald and his wife finally came down the stairs. As they reached the ground floor, Gerald said reluctantly, "I am late for an appointment with my man of business. But remember, my love, you have promised to ask your artist when it will be possible for me to see the portrait."

"I will, but . . . since it is in the library, I expect it would not hurt if you looked at it. We would not have to tell him."

"And what about that complicated cloth?"

"We could probably put it back were we to pay close attention to the folds."

"No, we will not try. I have given my word that I will not. One does have to humor artists. They are a strange breed, do you not agree?"

"Monsieur de Beaufort can be a little short-tempered, I think."

"I hope you will not tell me that he has exercised that temper on you." Gerald frowned.

"No, of course not," she assured him. "However, he is inclined to rail at his brushes and the paints—quite as if they had conspired against him. But, of course, I do understand that."

"Do you?" he asked curiously. "I cannot say that I do."

"You would if you wrote or painted. If you spill ink or make a smear where you had aimed a thin stroke, you are inclined to blame everything except yourself."

He laughed. "I see. It is a characteristic peculiar to the artistic temperament."

"Very peculiar." She laughed.

"I will have to agree with that." He smiled, even though he was not quite pleased to find his wife so understanding of the artist's peculiarities. Still, he was fair enough to recognize the reasons for his displeasure, if he could use so strong a term.

Chrétien de Beaufort had been recommended by Felice. Did that mean that the man was aware of their relationship? And if he were aware of it, would he pass that information on to Belinda? Gerald shuddered at the notion. Still, he did not believe he had much to fear from that quarter. Undoubtedly the artist wanted to collect the large sum he had asked for the portrait, and judging from his shabby garments, he needed it. He would not do anything to jeopardize his payments. The

French were notoriously thrifty. Consequently, Gerald shrugged that fear away.

Soon after Gerald's departure, Chrétien arrived. He came into an unoccupied library and looked about him with considerable pleasure. On this morning, he was particularly pleased about a habit he had developed over the years. As he was careful to tell each new client, he needed at least a half-hour to work himself into the mood for painting. It was true, of course, that he needed to be in a mood for his work, but it was also true that this particular request served to increase his clients' respect for his talents.

On this morning, which marked the next-to-last of Belinda's sittings, he was of two minds. He had received a goodly sum in advance for his work, but he had yet to collect the rest. However, if he did not receive it, there were other commissions awaiting him. There always were. Furthermore, his passion for Belinda exceeded anything he had ever experienced for the females who came so easily into his arms—excepting only one.

He sighed and tried not to dwell on that one whom he had loved for a long time and still loved—but hopes engendered by Napoleon's Russian misadventures precluded that relationship. He had that in common with Gerald—a nobleman of France could not wed the offspring of a scenic designer and her lover—and had he become truly involved with Felice, he knew full well that, unlike Gerald, damn his eyes, he would never have had the strength to leave her.

Belinda was a different matter entirely. She admired his work and he had a strong feeling that she admired him too, even though she had cleverly never given him any indication of those feelings. All that could be changed. He wanted it to be changed. He would be killing two birds with one stone, and that pleased him.

He moved to the shelves, hoping that the book he had placed there the previous day still remained in the same spot. As he had anticipated, it had not been moved. The young inhabitants of this lordly house were not, at this time, given to frequenting the library. He took the volume off the shelf and slipped a little ivory oval inside. Then, pulling a cord, he asked the servant who answered his summons to tell her ladyship that he was awaiting her.

As the man left the room, Chrétien smiled. Then his smile vanished as he thought of Felice and the hurt she had suffered and was still suffering at the hands of the young man who had so cruelly and casually broken her heart. A little thrill of anger went through him as he remembered those anguished moments in her studio. Felice was very, very dear to him, but he must not dwell on that now. He must think of this beautiful and inexperienced child—to whom he would soon be dealing a very cruel blow. He hoped that she would not be too despairing to accept the comfort he had to offer her, comfort which would more than compensate her for her husband's defection.

A tap on the door scattered his thoughts. His eyes glistened. The time for which he had planned was finally upon him. He rose swiftly and hurried to open the door. "Ah, *bonjour*, your ladyship," he said with a warm smile. "Pray come in."

"Good morning, Monsieur de Beaufort. You are ready for me, then?" Belinda asked shyly as she came inside.

"I am quite ready." He nodded, wondering if she were in the least aware of how very provocative her remark had been. He doubted it. She was not yet in full command of her power to enchant. Still, she was looking ravishing, he thought jealously. She had the dreaming gaze of a woman who has been awakened by her lover's kiss. Women did possess a very special aura when they were deep in the throes of their first love and were deeply loved in return.

He had surprised a similar expression on Felice's face when she had been with Gerald. Damn the rogue! He little deserved the love he had awakened in either woman's breast. However, now was not the time to think of that. He must concentrate upon the task at hand.

"I hope you have rested enough, Monsieur de Beaufort," she said.

"I have that, milady," he replied. "Indeed, I might have started sooner, but I have been whiling away the time by reading this book of verse. It is justly famous." He held it up and was pleased to see the little scrap of ivory fall to the floor between them. He was further pleased to discover that it had fallen face-upward. He immediately retrieved it, looking at it with well-assumed surprise. "But . . . but what could this be doing here?" he questioned.

"It . . . it is a miniature," she said. "Might I see it, please?"

"But of course." He started to hand it to her, and then stopped. *"Mais, qu'est-ce que ça?"* He turned an astonished face in the direction of Belinda. "But I know the lady." He handed the miniature to her.

"Do you?" Belinda stared at the pictured face. "She is certainly very beautiful."

"And I assure you that she did not flatter herself," he said.

"I . . . do not understand."

"It is a self-portrait of Mademoiselle Felice D'Aubigny. She, too, is an artist. She makes her living painting these miniatures. I wonder what it was doing in your book."

"I cannot imagine," Belinda said. "You know her, you say?"

He nodded. "I know her quite well, milady. Indeed, I owe her a great deal, for it was she who recommended my work to Lord Courtenay, but, of course, that is why she is in this book. I expect your husband meant to frame it, but he forgot where he put it."

"My husband knows the lady . . . well?" Belinda asked.

"Oh, yes. Am I to understand that he did not tell you it was Mademoiselle D'Aubigny who recommended me?"

"I . . . I expect it must have slipped his

mind," Belinda said. "I have not heard the lady's name until today."

He looked flustered. "Oh? Have you not?"

"Who is Felice D'Aubigny?" she demanded, and then, staring at the miniature, she added, "But I . . . I think I know her work. I received a miniature of my husband . . . before we married. It was sent to my aunt. I wonder . . ."

"Oh, yes, I am sure she painted it. She has been the good friend of your husband for . . . But I am not sure how long they have known each other." He smiled at Belinda and was pleased to see the color draining from her cheeks and the glow leaving her eyes as she put two and two together and realized the significance of the miniature in the book. She stared at the slip of ivory. "She is quite young, I think."

"She is twenty-three—she was a child of five when she was spirited out of France, poor little one. She lost everything. She is of noble birth, but she has been making her living with these trifles since she was fifteen. It has been very difficult for her—but fortunately, she is beautiful and can be very accommodating, as well."

"I see." Belinda nodded.

She appeared stricken and, as he had hoped she might, she suddenly picked up the book and looked at it. "*The Love Sonnets* of Ronsard," she said, and put it down quickly.

"Yes, it is an excellent translation . . . though nothing can quite equal the original French. But enough, my dear Lady Courtenay, shall we begin work?"

"Yes, if you please," she said dully.

As she went to her chair, Chrétien was further pleased to note that all the spontaneity had gone from her walk. She moved slowly and her shoulders drooped.

The knowledge that he had been recommended by her husband's mistress had, as he had hoped, not taken long to seep into her active little mind. He would not press his advantage at this time, however. There would be one more sitting, and then . . . He would see. Still, there was also a very large chance that he would not see—because were she to tell her husband about the miniature, he might easily perceive the plot—but he would also get tangled in explanations and ultimately betray himself. Chrétien vanquished a burgeoning smile and picked up his palette and his brushes.

Gerald had a mistress. The mistress had recommended the artist who was painting her. Gerald loved his mistress. He kept her likeness in a book of love poems she might never have seen had not Monsieur de Beaufort been reading it. Gerald's mistress was very beautiful. And when he was not with his wife, was he with this woman? Of course! And when he was not with this woman, he read love poems and fondled her miniature, and as for herself, his pretense of feeling was masterly, but it was pretense. Belinda, lying on her chaise longue as these thoughts circulated through her mind, put her hand to her heart and found it beating strongly, showing that its breakage was only figurative. But broken it was.

What can I do? she thought.

She sat up straight and put a hand to that damaged heart, wondering why, since it was broken, it was not aching. Hearts were reputed to ache at times like these but, again, an aching heart was only a figure of speech. And now, suddenly, she was angry! Indeed, in the space of a second, her anger was akin to fury. She had been vilely traduced by Gerald and his mistress—by his mistress and her lover, who was Gerald. That accounted for the coldness that had existed at the beginning of their marriage! He had not wanted to marry her and she had not wanted to marry him, she recalled. The marriage had been forced upon her. The marriage had been forced upon him too. And why? He needed an heir!

However, at first he had evaded his responsibilities. He had absented himself very often. He had pleaded appointments with his man of business—but his "man" had been a woman, her name Felice D'Aubigny! Then, belatedly remembering the reason he had married her, he had decided to try and make the best of it. Those efforts had begun at Vauxhall, when he had shown what she had foolishly imagined to be signs of love for her. He did not love her. He only wanted to oblige his family and get his wife with child!

He ought to have been an actor, she thought bitterly. He would have been a splendid actor. Oh, God, I cannot stay with him!

No, of course she could not, but until she

could find a way to leave him, she must needs keep her anger and her thoughts to herself. Any notion of repeating the artist's confidences to her husband must be put aside. Naturally, he would have denied the allegations, and she did not want to listen to those vain excuses.

She would bide her time and then she would leave. After her departure, Gerald would receive a letter, but until she had gone . . . She would enclose that missive in the volume of poetry, Ronsard's love poetry. She would also enclose the miniature therein. He would not want to lose it.

Meanwhile, her plans must be carefully made. Would she have to suffer his pretended caresses until she could get away? No, no, no, she would plead a headache or a stomachache or a chill—or all three, together. Perhaps he would imagine that his purpose had been accomplished and she was with child. He deserved that particular delusion, but no, no, no, she would not pretend to it. She did not want to give him that satisfaction and she did not want him hovering over her with his false smiles and his false words of endearment and his false caresses. The less she saw of her betrayer, the better it would be.

6

Belinda lay in bed moaning as Mary solicitously massaged her temples. Standing at the foot of the bed, Gerald regarded her anxiously. Indeed, Belinda thought bitterly, he appeared to be the very epitome of husbandly concern. However, she could also remember her father hovering over her mother's couch with much the same expression written large upon his face as he regretfully discussed the business that necessitated his immediate journey to London, the "business" who had been performing a leading role in a revival of *The Beggar's Opera* at Drury Lane. In imitation of her mother's actions at that time, Belinda closed her eyes and moaned.

Gerald said disappointedly, "I must go out of town briefly, my dearest. I will be back by the week's end at the latest."

"Must you go?" Belinda whispered in direct imitation of her mother.

"Yes." He managed an artful sigh. "I have already made arrangements. I am very sorry that you cannot come with me, my love."

Had her father said something like that? Yes, she recalled wryly, he had—using practically the same words. He, too, had sighed, with equal artistry. She whispered, "I am sorry too, but perhaps next time, Gerald dearest." She had difficulty quelling a threatening smile as she envisioned his shock when he returned and found her gone. Then, as he bent to kiss her, she steeled herself to suffer that unwanted caress, guessing that, given her oft-mentioned malady, he would not question her lack of response.

"I pray you will soon be yourself again, my dearest." He did give her another anxious and, she thought, an admirable imitation of a hurt look. Then he left.

Belinda saw him out gladly. It had been very difficult for her to keep her angry thoughts to herself, very difficult not to reveal what she had learned. And perhaps, if she would not have jeopardized Monsieur de Beaufort, she might have flung the name of Felice D'Aubigny in his face. There had been moments when it had danced upon her tongue, actually begging to be uttered, but she had swallowed it and forced the smile with which she had sent him forth and, most likely, into the waiting arms of his lovely French mistress!

"But milady, are you sure you feel well enough to go?" Mary, standing in the middle of the dressing room, regarded her mistress anxiously.

"Please help me finish dressing, Mary," Belinda said more crisply than was her wont

in speaking to her abigail. "After all, I have
spent most of the day in bed. Consequently, I
find that I am feeling much more the thing.
Besides, I have promised Lady Evelyn that I
will go. I will return in good time, I assure
you." She was aware of Mary's disconcerted
gaze, and no doubt the servants' quarters
would be rife with gossip, some of which
would surely find its way into his lordship's
ears. However, by the time Gerald heard it,
she would not be here.

Lady Evelyn Mainwaring was one of Belinda's
new London acquaintances, a charming young
woman who had known Gerald since, she
was fond of saying, they had both been in
leading strings. Shortly after meeting Belinda,
she had confided that she was glad of her
influence on Gerry, because he truly needed
to be domesticated. Since she had not enlarged upon the subject, Belinda was now
positive that she had been making an elliptical reference to his artistic mistress. She
hoped that on this night she would be able to
corner her hostess and sound her out on the
subject of Mlle. D'Aubigny.

Unfortunately, when she arrived, Lady Evelyn, after complimenting Belinda on her new
and ravishing turquoise-and-gold gown and
the aquamarine-and-gold necklace and tiara,
Gerald's latest gift, vanished from her side
and was currently flitting around the vast
drawing room like a bee confronted with a
paucity of nectar. As was her wont, she never
stayed long enough to finish a conversation
with any of her guests.

There was to be a musicale that night. A soprano and a mezzo-soprano from the Royal Opera would be singing selections from Gluck's opera *Orpheus et Euridice*. Consequently, Lady Evelyn fluttered at Belinda's side once more as she indicated a group of spindly chairs, some already occupied by her guests. She was about to direct Belinda to an unoccupied seat in the second row when Lord Furneaux suddenly rose up from one of those chairs.

"Oh, gracious, Anthony, you did startle me, rising up like a deer affrighted. You know Lady Belinda, do you not . . . shall I place you side by side? Or is that chair reserved?"

Belinda, her startled gaze on Lord Furneaux's face, waited almost breathlessly for his response, and exhaled a caught breath when his lordship smiled and bowed. "Belinda, my dear, well met by candlelight, to paraphrase the bard."

"Lord Furneaux." Belinda held out her hand and smiled at him as he bore it to his lips.

"May I place her beside you, Anthony?" Lady Evelyn repeated.

"Of course, my dear. Belinda and I are old friends."

"Indeed, well . . . I must see to everyone, must not keep the musicians waiting, strange sort . . . instrumentalists, singers too, you know." She hurried away.

"But this is certainly an unexpected pleasure." Lord Furneaux smiled at Belinda.

"It is unexpected for me too," she assured him.

"And where is Gerald?" he inquired. "I trust that he will soon be joining us?"

"No, he will not," she said in a hard little voice. "He is out of town. I came by myself. I . . . I did not wish to disappoint Lady Evelyn."

"I see." He regarded her quizzically. "But should you have come here unaccompanied, my dear?"

"I expect not, but . . . but I wanted to hear the music."

"I see." He nodded.

"No, I do not expect that you do, Lord . . . Anthony." Belinda lowered her voice as she continued passionately, "Oh, Anthony, I imagine you are shocked to see me here without my husband, and might even be wondering why I did not accompany him from London. I am positive that he is wondering the same thing. Still, if I might presume upon the fact that we have known each other for years, even if those years have not followed one upon the next, may I please explain myself?"

He looked surprised and concerned. "Of course, my dear child. I am naturally anxious to know what is troubling you."

"I . . . I am determined to leave London and . . . and go home. Oh, Ant . . . oh, Lord Furneaux, if you do not have anything better to do, would you . . . would you please take me to the country?" The moment those impassioned words left her lips, she shuddered at her daring. "I . . . I mean . . ."

"I am sure that you mean exactly what you have just said, my child," he responded quickly.

"We will talk later, and you will tell me the rest, of course."

"You . . . you will talk with me . . . you promise?" she whispered.

"Have I not just said so?" He put his warm fingers over her two small clenched hands. "Indeed, I will contrive to spirit you away from this gathering as soon as it is polite to do so."

"Oh, I would be so grateful," she whispered.

"You do not need to be grateful, child. I will do anything in my power to help you," he murmured. Then, as the musicians and the singers, a pair of enormously heavy women in white Grecian robes that made them look even heavier, entered, Lord Furneaux, with a slight shudder, defensively closed his eyes. As the music began, he gave every evidence of being deeply asleep, but as the first group of arias ended, he quickly arose, and helping Belinda to her feet, drew her out of the chamber and subsequently led her into the moonlit garden, saying firmly, "I know a spot where we will not be disturbed, my dear."

"You are so very kind. I hope you will not mind missing the rest of the program."

He smiled down at her. "Might I confess to you that I cannot envision a feminine Orpheus, and it is even more difficult to watch a Euridice who would have considerable trouble squeezing into Charon's skiff. In fact, I am not at all sure that she would not be engulfed in the waters of Lethe, long before her husband came to redeem her."

Belinda could not repress a giggle. "That was most unkind, my lord," she chided.

"Not if it could make you laugh, my dear. Now, come . . ." He led her to a little marble folly at the end of the garden, and indicating a stone bench, bade her sit down. As she did, he sat beside her, slipping a comforting arm around her waist. "Now, I beg you will acquaint me with your problem. Perhaps I will be able to suggest a solution."

Belinda shook her head. "No," she told him dolefully, "there are some problems that do not have solutions."

"That, my dear child, is against the laws of mathematics," he said.

Belinda had not meant to weep, but by the time she had finished her tale of betrayal, her face was wet with tears. "You see . . ." she sobbed. "There is no solution, none at all. I will have to leave him."

Her hearer changed his arm from her waist to her shoulders and pulled her against him. "My dearest, why did you not ask him for an explanation?"

She shook her head. "What could he have said?" she sobbed.

"My dear, quite truthfully, I cannot imagine that with you for a bride, he would have continued this liaison. I have a feeling that some mistake has been made."

"There was no mistake," Belinda said stubbornly. "There was the same signature on the miniature that was sent to me. It was *her* work . . . she painted her lover so that his bride would have his likeness. She painted herself so that her lover would have her likeness. And he . . . he put it in a book of love poems to . . . to mark his place. I might t-tell you that that book shows signs of use. The page was much dog-eared where her portrait lay."

"But, my dearest child, this is all conjecture," he said insistently.

"I wish it were, but the artist . . . Monsieur de Beaufort has known her for a long time. He . . . he has her confidence. Gerald was with her before he married me."

"But you would not have expected him to live a . . . life of celibacy, my dearest Belinda. He . . . all of us have a period in our lives when we sow wild oats."

"But do you press those wild oats between the pages of a book? Do you sit and read it and think about your m-mistress, while your w-wife is in the next room?" Belinda raised her streaming eyes. "I want to go home, Lord Furneaux. Will you p-please take me home?"

"Yes, of course," he said quickly. "I am sure your hostess will understand that you are not well, my dear. I will order my post chaise."

"I do not mean here in London," she said quickly. "P-please take me to my mother, my poor mother, whose anguish I now understand! Take me now . . . while Gerald is away. I do not want to be home when he returns. I never, never want to see him again. Please, my lord, help me in this. . . ."

"I am at your service, of course, my dear, but—"

"Then, if you are, I pray that you will help me!" Belinda cried.

Lord Furneaux, looking down into Belinda's pleading, tearstained face, found himself feeling very sorry for her. He had always had a soft corner for this lovely child. Still, at the same time, he was annoyed. His annoyance was directed at Gerald, who had certainly been foolish, leaving his mistress's portrait in a book of love poems. What on earth had possessed the young cub? he wondered angrily. Looking down into Belinda's moon-gilded face, he was even more annoyed. She was beautiful, even with her eyes abrim with tears. In addition to that, she was intelligent and sweet-natured, and having seen the pair together, he did not doubt that Gerald was aware of these assets. However, the marriage had not been made in heaven. It had been a cut-and-dried arrangement between parents, and with a different bridegroom in mind.

It was quite possible that Gerald might have waxed extremely resentful over their arbitrary decision. There was no doubt that the boy had a mistress. He himself had seen Gerald with the lovely Felice. It was natural that he would have entertained certain regrets upon entering the married state. However, seeing them dancing together that night at Vauxhall Gardens, he had been quite sure that Gerald was becoming accustomed to his marriage. More than merely accustomed. The lad had looked absolutely mesmerized! Yet, certainly it had been foolish for him to leave that book lying about. It was possible that he needed a lesson, and if Belinda were to leave . . .

"You will not help me," Belinda said with a catch in her voice. "I . . . I had best go in."

"We had best both go in," he said. "However, I *will* help you, my dear. I will take you anywhere you wish to go."

"Oh, my lord," Belinda cried, and flung her arms around him. "Oh, I do thank you."

He gently separated himself from her clinging embrace. "I have certain matters that require my attention, my dear. But I believe that I will be able to go . . . say, the day after tomorrow?" He frowned. "No, it had best be Friday."

"He promised you that?" Cornelia looked at Belinda, her amazement tinged with anger.

"He did." Belinda nodded. "We will leave on Friday."

"You and . . . and Lord Furneaux, alone?" Cornelia asked incredulously. "But you cannot . . ."

Belinda regarded her friend with a touch of hauteur. "I can and I will," she said distinctly. "He will take me to . . . to my home."

"That is a three-day journey, at least," Cornelia said in shocked accents. "You cannot remain in Lord Furneaux's company for three mortal days! You . . . you will be ruined!"

"I trust him. I have known him practically my whole life. He . . . he could be my father," Belinda cried. She added mulishly, "I will not stay in Gerald's house any longer than is absolutely necessary. I will not remain with a

man who has betrayed me, who has his mistress's picture in a book of love poems, and
who employed Monsieur de Beaufort on her
recommendation and has been s-seeing her
all the t-time he has been p-pretending that
he loves me."

"I have often seen you together, my dear,
and I certainly never had the impression that
Gerald was *pretending* to love you! He cannot
take his eyes off you . . . he obviously adores
you."

"Stuff and nonsense!" Belinda retorted hotly.
"If he loved me, he would not still be visiting
his mistress. Monsieur de Beaufort has told
me he has met him there . . . often."

"Damn the man!" Cornelia exclaimed with
uncharacteristic rage. "Why could he not
have kept his mouth shut when he saw the
picture?"

"I expect he was surprised . . ."

"And then to tell you who it was recommended him . . ." Cornelia snapped. "If you
wish to know what I think, I think you should
wait until Gerald comes home and receive an
explanation from him as well."

"I will not wait. I do not want to wait. I do
not want to speak to him ever, ever, ever
again," Belinda wailed. She brushed a hand
across her tearing eyes. "I want to go h-home
to poor Mama . . . Mama, who has suffered
as I am suffering now."

"And that, then, is your last word on the
subject?" Cornelia demanded.

"It is!" Belinda lifted her chin. "And I must
say, Cornelia, I thought that you of all peo-

ple, you, my very best friend, would have been more understanding."

"I am understanding," Cornelia said crossly. "I understand, for instance, that you will be making a great cake of yourself if you persist on journeying all the way to Somerset in the company of an unmarried gentleman!"

"He is not unmarried!" Belinda stamped her foot. "He is a widower and he is thirty-seven!"

"He is still single, and a thirty-seven-year-old man is not a hoary ancient, as you seem to imagine! God knows how many females have been casting out lures for Lord Furneaux and would be glad if he but looked at them! Futhermore, he does not look anywhere near thirty-seven, and if you go with him, you will be ruined and Gerald will be entirely within his rights if he divorces you. It would serve you right, Belinda."

"I want him to divorce me!" Belinda glared at Cornelia. "I do not want to be married to . . . to a man who . . . who has a . . . a mistress and k-keeps her p-picture in a b-book of l-love poetry. I . . . I feel besmirched."

"It is she who is besmirched, not you," Cornelia snapped. "You, however, will be totally besmirched if you persist in this mad scheme."

"I have told you that I do not care!" Belinda cried hotly. "I wish to leave. I wish to leave before Gerald returns. I do not want to see him ever, ever again," Belinda retorted, emphasizing each "ever" with a stamp of her foot. "He has b-broken my heart."

"And that is your last word on the subject?"

"It is my last word. I am going, Cornelia. I am going on the appointed day—tomorrow—and I do not give two figs for anything anyone might say, so there."

"Very well, Belinda, so be it!" Cornelia snapped. "But I, for one, think you have gone mad."

"I do not care what you think, Cornelia!" Belinda turned her back on her friend and ran from the room. In another few moments she had left the house. And in yet another few moments, Lady Elizabeth being in the garden and unaware of this stormy confrontation, Cornelia had also left the house, though she did not go in the same direction as her outraged friend.

Informed that a Lady Hazzard wished to see him, a Lady Hazzard who was young and in quite a taking, Lord Furneaux mentally conjured up a series of feminine images and could not imagine why any of these would have come to his home. He did not immediately connect the name Hazzard with anyone he knew. However, his curiosity was piqued, and though entirely aware that he might regret it, he said, "Very well, Edwards. Please show her into the drawing room."

"I have already done so, your lordship," the butler responded, further surprising his master. Evidently his unknown guest had made a most favorable impression on Edwards. Anthony had always trusted Edwards' judgment. His butler had never had any difficulty whatsoever in separating the wheat from the chaff.

His head full of conjecture concerning the identity of his visitor, he strode into the drawing room and stopped short as he recognized Lady Cornelia. She had been standing by the window, but as he entered, she had whirled to face him, her face much flushed and her eyes full of an anger that verged on fury. Without preamble, she said sharply, "You, a man of the world, Lord Furneaux, how could you not realize that she is an innocent? Yes, even though she is married, she is certainly not up to snuff! In these circumstances, how could you contemplate such a thing? It passes all understanding!"

He regarded her confusedly. "I am not sure that I know whom you are talking about, Lady Cornelia."

She actually stamped her foot. "I am talking about Belinda," she snapped. "And I might tell you that she is absolutely determined on going with you tomorrow, even though I have told her that it is the most arrant folly, especially with a man of your reputation!" Then she suddenly blushed deeply. "Oh, d-dear," she said belatedly. "I . . . I meant . . ."

A smile played about his well-shaped mouth. His golden eyes gleamed with amusement now. He said, "You have stated your meaning most precisely, my dear Lady Cornelia. I trust you are referring to Lady Belinda's journey to Somerset."

"Yes," she acknowledged in a small voice. "But I did not intend to . . . to . . ." She

suddenly burst out, "It is just that she is
being so headstrong and . . . and foolish. And
there is something about the tale that does
not ring quite true. It is my opinion that she
should wait to hear Gerald's side, but she
absolutely refuses."

"I beg you will sit down, Lady Cornelia," he
said gently as he indicated a chair.

She shook her head. "I should not have
come here. It was just that . . . that—"

"Now that you are here," he broke into her
embarrassed rush of excuses, "I insist that
you sit down. There." He pointed to the chair.
"Please, my dear," he added.

Still blushing and deeply embarrassed, she
obeyed. "I did not mean . . ." she began.

He drew up a chair and sat down facing
her. "I must tell you, my dear Lady Cornelia,
that I had no intention of escorting Belinda
to Somerset unless there were a chaperone in
attendance. I have been racking my brains as
to how I might find one upon whose discre-
tion I could depend. However, thus far I have
been unsuccessful, and was . . . er . . . gird-
ing my loins to tell Belinda that I could not
be of service to her. You, however, could act
in that capacity. You would be an excellent
chaperone."

"I?" Cornelia regarded him in amazement.
"But—" she began.

"Heed me, I beg of you," he said hastily. "I
know you are young, and there is your reputation to be guarded as well. You must know
that I have it in mind to stay at less popular
inns and to take every precaution that we

will not be recognized by those travelers with whom we might be acquainted. Furthermore, though I am unmarried and, possibly a bit of a rake . . ."

"Oh, my lord," Cornelia protested almost tearfully, "I . . . I meant only that . . ."

He raised his hand. "I must confess to you, my dear Lady Cornelia, that much of what you have told me is unfortunately accurate. I do not have an unblemished reputation. Still, I can assure you that my intentions regarding Belinda are entirely honorable. Furthermore, I am reasonably sure that a man with two young ladies in his care could hardly be suspected of seduction. In fact, I happen to think he would be believed were he to say that they were his nieces. He has it in mind to further allay gossip by remaining at one inn while his nieces put up at another. Would that satisfy your strong sense of propriety, my dear Lady Cornelia?"

She was silent a moment, mulling over this extraordinary proposal. She said finally, "I think it would, my lord, but still I believe that Belinda should wait to see Gerald. I am of the opinion that he adores her."

"I am rather sure of that myself. I also have a strong suspicion that Belinda, whom I have known since she was in short clothes, will leave him a note telling him of her intentions and I would not be surprised were she to describe our route. If he catches up with us and proposes a duel, I will refuse to fight him."

"Please . . ." She looked at him anxiously.

"I hope she does not leave a note. You could be hurt."

He regarded her quizzically. "I am not worried about that, my dear Lady Cornelia, but I do thank you for your concern."

She frowned and said insistently, "You can never be sure. Someone I knew, who was similarly sure of himself and a master of swordplay, died in a duel."

"I am sorry for that, my dear." He studied her face. "I believe he must have been a good friend."

Cornelia looked down. "We . . . grew up together," she said softly. "Our parents visited back and forth, they were neighbors. Our estates marched with each other. It . . . it was a long time ago."

"I cannot think it was too long ago," he said.

"I was fifteen when it happened. I am twenty now."

"That is certainly not a great age, my dear Lady Cornelia. Am I to understand that you are still wearing the willow?"

Cornelia, meeting a sympathetic and probing gaze, flushed. "No, not anymore. At the time I was much cast down, but now I remember only the good times we used to have and how he could make me laugh. He was full of laughter himself . . . though he was rather too prone to practical jokes. He . . . he died too young. He was only eighteen."

"He died in a duel, you say?" Lord Furneaux frowned. "Who would wantonly slay an eighteen-year-old?"

" 'Twas another of his own age. I do not know why they fought—but the one who killed him ran away to war. He died in Spain."

"Spain . . ." Lord Furneaux sighed and shook his head. "These useless wars fought out of ambition and a desire for personal glory, costing French lives as well as English . . ."

"And so very many in Russia." Cornelia shuddered.

"Yes . . . but enough, let us turn our minds to the present, my dear. And you must let me escort you home."

"That is not necessary, my lord," she said quickly. "I have come by post chaise and my abigail is waiting for me."

"Ah." He smiled. "I am glad that you were not foolish enough to venture into the dragon's lair without protection. You are truly a very sensible young woman."

She gave him a long look. "I do not think of you as a dragon, my lord."

"Nor should you." He laughed. "I think I will look forward to this cross-country jaunt, you know, if only for your alleviating presence. Together we must do our best to keep up poor Belinda's spirits . . . even though I, for one, happen to believe that it is a tempest in a teapot."

"I do hope so," she said feelingly. Then she flushed. "I must beg your pardon for coming here like . . ." She hesitated as he held up his hand.

"Do not beg my pardon, my dear Lady Cornelia. You are a good friend to Belinda, and as for myself, I have enjoyed our conversation and I will look forward to your presence on our journey. However, I will, of course, discuss this matter with Lady Elizabeth, who is my good friend." He paused, staring at her. "I think that alarms you. Why?"

"N-no," Cornelia stammered. "I . . . I mean . . . I hardly think she would approve my coming here . . ."

"But you did not come here, my dear," he said smoothly. "I met you at the house of a friend. Whom have you visited this week?"

"Lady Fortescue and—"

"Ah," he interrupted. "I know her very well. We met there and you confided your fears to me and I have proposed this solution. I promise you that I will sustain no arguments from our Belinda, who might not see the need for a chaperone. Are you easier in your mind, my dear?"

Cornelia flushed. "I did not really believe . . ." she began regretfully.

He held up a hand again. "Enough, my dear. You were right to be uneasy. You are a true friend to Belinda, and while we know each other, you and I, we are not intimates. Consequently, may I say that I look forward to allaying your well-justified fears?"

"They are entirely allayed, my lord," she hastened to assure him. "And I do thank you."

He gave her a long and, to her mind, inscrutable look. "I thank you for coming, Lady Cornelia. I will see you out."

Once back in the post chaise, Cornelia found herself strangely excited. Indeed, his kind-

ness had more than made up for that evening at Vauxhall when she had seen him
with his pretty little mistress and sustained
a disappointment which she had tried most
unsuccessfully to put behind her. It had been
the memory of that girl that had occasioned
those words she still longed to call back. Yet,
seemingly, he had not taken them amiss—as
another man might easily have done. He . . .
But she had not to dwell on him. She must
make plans to leave the city, and she would
have to take her plainest garments—though
it might not hurt to include her blue lutestring:
she did look her best in blue. Then, as she
realized the direction in which her thoughts
were tending, she blushed and quickly
banished them. Lord Furneaux was kind and
she must be very careful not to mistake his
intrinsic kindness for anything else. As all
the polite world was quite aware, he had put
love behind him.

7

On the morning of her departure from her husband's house, Belinda, who had scarcely slept the previous night, was half-excited, half-miserable as her imagination presented her with a panorama of her future life, which, after the divorce, would necessarily be lived in seclusion and most likely in her parents' house. She would be the outcast to whom no one referred. In time, she would be the elderly aunt who might be allowed to see her nephews and nieces—but probably not until they were grown. Meanwhile, she could occupy herself in good works to expiate a sin that was not of her committing—but that would not matter.

A divorced woman, guilty or not guilty, had no entrée to society. She was judged to have a concupiscent nature and she lived in the equivalent of an eternal twilight, unless, of course, she chose to disgrace herself further and have a series of affairs. That would be her only alternative, because no one would marry her because there would be no dowry.

Even if her husband returned the monies to her father, they would be included in the dowry of her younger sister. And, she reminded herself swiftly, she would not want to marry again unless . . . She frowned, wishing for the hundredth time that Lord Furneaux had not invited Cornelia to come with them. She had hoped that were she alone with Lord Furneaux, whom she had always adored . . . But she could not dwell upon these hopes, for Cornelia, interfering Cornelia, had scotched them! She had gone to see Lord Furneaux at his house, a very daring thing to do and utterly unlike shy, proper Cornelia! She had, in effect, gone to save Belinda's reputation!

Belinda groaned. If she and Lord Furneaux might have been alone . . . But, alas, he had readily agreed to Cornelia's suggestion, or rather her interference, her unwarranted interference, and he had said he had wanted a chaperone all along. However, if Cornelia had not interfered, he might have been of quite a different mind! She sighed, and though it would be fully three hours before Lord Furneaux arrived, she rang for her abigail.

When she was dressed and ready, Belinda went down to the library and looked once more at the book of poems and the miniature. She had left them on the desk, prominently displayed. She had intended that these two objects speak for themselves. However, since there was plenty of time, she decided that after all, she would include a note—the better to clarify her intentions and express her feelings.

The note took rather longer than she had anticipated, and by the time she laid down her pen, it occupied three closely written sheets of paper and was, she thought, quite well-expressed. In fact, when she was going over the miseries attendant upon divorce, she had quite forgotten her writing. She could write. She would write novels and send them to the Minerva Press, and her first would concern her husband and his mistress. It should make for very good reading. She folded the note or, rather, the letter, and put it in the book, blinking away the tears that were blurring her sight.

She had done a great deal of reading in the last week, and her eyes were strained. Consequently, they were tearing. She decided that she would not try to read on her way to her parents' home. It was next to impossible to read in a moving coach and, of course, Cornelia would be at her side and she would want to converse. She grimaced. She did not feel like talking to her friend, but still, it would be lovely to be away. In fact, she could hardly wait until it was nine o'clock. They would be taking the long journey in easy stages. There was certainly no reason to rush. Gerald would not be home until tomorrow, and it was unlikely that he would want to pursue them. Indeed, happily free from the encumbrance of an unwanted wife, he would go immediately to his mistress's house and . . . But she forbore to dwell upon what he would do once he arrived. Her eyes were really bothering her; they needed immediate attention, and she had forgotten to bring a handkerchief. She hurried out of the library and dashed up the stairs.

The door was shaking under loud, rapid knocks. Felice, who had been working, hastily put down her brushes and hurried to open it. She was not surprised to find a pale and furious Gerald standing just beyond the threshold. In no more than a second he was across the threshold, and if she had not stepped back just as quickly, he would have knocked her down. Judging from his expression, she suspected that this might have been his intent.

Given what she knew about Chrétien's stratagem, she had been anticipating a visit from Gerald. Yet she had also thought that he would have gone to Chrétien's studio rather than coming here. That did not matter! He was here, and the look on his face both surprised her and put her on her guard. In the course of their relationship she had seen him in many moods, not excluding anger, but this was not anger. It appeared to be compounded of many moods—rage, misery, and accusation. And, she realized with an inner shiver, he actually looked murderous. Despite that inner trepidation, she managed to say calmly, "What is the meaning of this . . . intrusion, Gerald?"

He glared at her. In a tight, constricted tone of voice he said, "Where is he?"

"Who?" She stared at him blankly. "I do not know—"

"I am talking about your damned paramour," he yelled. "Where is he? Did you put him up to this?" He held up a leather-bound book and then hurled it against the opposite wall, where it fell to the floor, a mass of pages spilling out of its shattered binding. He held up the miniature. "Did you paint this for my wife's edification, damn you to hell?" He caught her by the shoulders, shaking her so roughly that her teeth closed hurtfully on her tongue. "Did you?" he demanded again. "Did you?"

Her fear increased. It seemed to her that Gerald had gone mad, but she must not let him see that she was afraid. She managed to gaze up at him coldly and to say in a frozen voice, "I do not know what you are talking about. I charge you, Gerald, release me! Release me at once! You are hurting me."

"Am I? I would like to break your damned neck." He hurled the words at her, the while his fingers, talonlike, continued to dig hurtfully into her arms. "I want to know who played this scurvy trick on my wife. Who was it told her that I was still sleeping with you? Who was it told her that we, you and I, had arranged that Chrétien paint her so that I might remain in touch with you without her suspecting the truth? It was you and that whoremaster you recommended, damn you!" He shook her roughly. "Was it not? And tell me where I can find him, or, by God, I will beat it out of you!"

"I can tell you nothing if you are determined on killing me, Gerald," she said coldly. "Dead lips do not give forth secrets."

He released her so suddenly that she lost her balance and fell in a heap at his feet. With an exclamation, he bent over her, and Felice, more frightened than she had ever been before, tried desperately to roll away. He caught her, and as she struggled to be free of him, he said quickly, "I am sorry . . . I did not mean to hurt you. I . . . I . . ." Tears suddenly filled his eyes. He helped her to her feet and moved away from her. "Oh, God, she has left me because . . . because she believes that you and I are still together. He told her . . . he showed her the miniature and the book . . . She . . . she did not even wait for my explanation. She has gone to . . . to Furneaux because she believes . . ." He turned toward Felice and seized her by the shoulders again. "This was your doing, it was you who put that damned artist up to telling my wife of our relationship, was it not?"

She glared up at him. "I said nothing to him. Anything he did, he did on his own."

"You knew when you brought him to my attention—" Gerald began.

"I knew only that you wanted a portrait painter!"

"You knew he would make love to her, damn you!"

"I knew nothing of the sort," she cried. "And perhaps you will be good enough to remember just why you wanted your wife's portrait painted—you wanted it done so that we—*we*—might have the time together!" Tears filled her eyes. "Anything that has happened rests on that . . . on your own folly, Gerald."

He groaned. "Yes, on my own folly. How was I to know that I would come to love her . . . how was I to know that I would come to worship her . . . and now . . . now she has gone."

"Did she say where?" Felice asked in a softer tone of voice.

"She said that she was going home."

"Then, Gerald, my dear, I suggest that you follow her."

"How can I make her believe . . . ?" he began hopelessly.

"I might tell you, Gerald, that a woman will believe anything she wishes to believe. If your wife truly loves you, she will, in time, believe you. Go after her, that is all I can suggest."

He sighed. "Very well, I shall. I hope . . ."

"I am sure that your hopes will be realized, Gerald. I wish you Godspeed."

He stared at her, seeming to see her, really see her, for the first time. "Oh, Felice, my dear," he said contritely. "I do not deserve such wishes from you." He moved toward her and was pained to see her shrink from him. "I will not hurt you," he assured her hastily. "I am sorry that I . . . I acted as I did. I am sorry that I led you to believe . . . I did not know that I would fall in love with her so very deeply. I think I went a little mad at the thought of losing her. Please forgive me."

She looked sadly up at him. "Very well, Gerald, I forgive you. And though I do not pretend to be a fortune-teller, I am quite sure that your wife will forgive you too, once she is apprised of the situation."

"I hope so," he sighed. He lifted her hand to his lips, and in a moment he was gone.

Felice sank down on her couch. Pushing back her sleeves, she looked at her arms. There were angry red marks on both of them, marks which would soon be black and blue. She grimaced. She had never seen Gerald in such a rage . . . and all because of that child he had married, that child who had effortlessly stolen him from her, and, unless she were deeply mistaken, had made an equally strong impression on Chrétien! For all that he had sworn he had acted in her behalf when he had formulated his hurtful scheme, she did not believe him. Chrétien had acted in his own behalf. Once he arrived at her studio, she would regale him with the tale of Gerald and the possible triumph of Lord Furneaux, who also appeared to be caught in the toils of this innocent enchantress!

In two days they had covered half the distance between London and Taunton, but as the afternoon wore on, a scattering of gray clouds was coalescing into an overall blanket of gray, hiding the blue and giving every indication of a rainstorm. A short time later, that rainstorm, coming down in huge drops, drove them into an inn outside the village of Codford St. Mary. One of the many hostelries bearing the name the King's Head, it was not very prepossessing but the increasing rain offered them little choice, and though Lord Furneaux told his two charges that he would find another inn for himself, they would not hear of it.

They were subsequently very glad of his presence as they came into the King's Head. Obviously they were not the first to have sought that particular sanctuary. The common room, located just off the main hall, was filled with travelers, and judging from the boisterous laughter that echoed through the hall, these worthies were in a most convivial mood. Mine host, a small, scruffy, shifty-eyed individual in an apron that was far from clean, welcomed his lordship and his nieces with obsequious bows and with much rubbing of his hands, as, nodding several times, he told them that they were in luck to have a suite on the second floor. Unfortunately, he did not have a single room for his lordship on that same floor, but there was a vacant chamber just above it.

Lord Furneaux frowned and glanced out of the window, grimacing as he saw that it was raining harder than ever. In a low voice he said, "I shall be just above you . . . and if there is any need to fetch me, you must send Mary. Do not come yourselves. Stay in your rooms. I do not like this place, but there is nothing to be done." In that moment his gaze hardened, and looking past them, he said coldly, "Is there anything that you find particularly interesting about us, sir?"

Cornelia, glancing in the direction he had turned, saw a tall man with a loose-lipped mouth and a most unpleasant grin, standing a few paces away. He visited a lowering look on Lord Furneaux, and without acknowledging his words, went sullenly back into the common room.

Without knowing quite why, Cornelia shivered. She turned to Lord Furneaux. "We will remain in our rooms, I assure you, my lord."

"Yes," Belinda agreed. "I . . . I do hope that the rain ceases before morning . . . the roads will be all mired."

"It usually does at this time of year," he said soothingly. He added, "I will not come up with you . . . we must avoid the appearance of evil."

Belinda, who had been looking very sober, bestowed a brief smile on him. "No one would ever believe you evil, my lord," she assured him quickly.

"No, indeed, they would not," Cornelia agreed softly.

"I am complimented." He sketched a slight bow.

A thin, guant young woman in a gray gown and a much-mended, not entirely clean white apron showed the girls to their suite. Its largest room was a medium-size chamber just a little wider than a large four-poster bed. A much-scratched armoire was shoved into one corner and a frayed and faded pink rug lay on the floor. A smaller room, not much larger than a closet, contained a cot obviously provided for the abigail. These two chambers opened onto a minute sitting room furnished with a battered deal table and two straight chairs with cane seats; there was also a sagging easy chair covered in cracked leather. A fire burning in a smoke-blackened fireplace was too small to provide adequate heating for the room or to allay the smell of mildew that coated the air. The rain, now coming down harder than ever, left black-edged streaks on a window facing the courtyard.

"Ugh!" Mary looked about her in disgust. "I'll warrant this window hasn't been cleaned since the last rain. And the rooms likewise."

"But," Cornelia said as brightly as she could, " 'tis only for the night."

Belinda, swallowing a burgeoning groan, agreed. "Yes, it is only for the night, Mary. And I expect we will feel better for a bit of supper."

"Yes, milady," the abigail said dubiously.

The chambermaid had come to stand beside the door leading into the hall. "Would there be anythin' else you'd be wantin'?" she asked.

"No, I'll be doin' for them," Mary told her quickly, and received a rather sullen, lowering look from the other girl.

"I'll be leavin' you, then." She bobbed a curtsy and withdrew.

"I will see to the unpacking," Mary said with a grimace she did not bother to conceal as she went into the bedroom.

Belinda, loosing a long sigh, sat down in one of the chairs near the table. "Oh, dear, rain seems to make everything so . . . so dampening."

"Yes, that cannot be denied," Cornelia agreed with a glint of laughter in her eyes.

Belinda also laughed, but quickly sobered. "I have heard of inns like this, but I never hoped to stay in one."

"I expect that we must be glad of a roof over our heads," Cornelia said bracingly.

"That is all it is—a roof." Belinda frowned. "And such a rowdy lot of men below."

"We'll not need to mix with them," Cornelia said comfortingly.

"You seem determined to make the best of it." Belinda rolled her eyes. "I expect I must too, but . . ." She looked down and added unhappily, "I wish . . ."

"What do you wish, my dearest?" Cornelia asked gently as Belinda sank into a gloomy silence.

"I wish . . ." she began, and then groaned. "But I could not have remained with him, not after seeing that book and . . . and the miniature," she said plaintively.

"I believe that if you had stayed to hear his side . . ." Cornelia began tentatively, and stopped as she met her friend's furious glare.

"He does not have a side!" Belinda cried. "If I could tell you the number of times he .. . he has closeted himself in that library, telling me that he had to . . . to go over reports from his man of business, when all along he was r-reading poetry and . . . and staring at *her* picture!"

"What he said was possibly true," Cornelia said insistently.

"It was not. I am sure he did exactly what I just told you he did." Belinda sobbed. "Just as I am equally positive that he is with her now." She went into the bedroom hastily, closing the door behind her.

"I beg you will not borrow trouble," Cornelia called after her a trifle impatiently.

In that moment there was a tap on the door. Cornelia, hurrying to open it, found the chambermaid outside. "Yes?" she asked.

"Beggin' yer pardon, milady, but the gentleman wot come wi' you wishes to see you," the girl murmured.

"He wants to see *me*?" Cornelia emphasized.

"Aye." The girl nodded. " 'E described you . . . said 'e'd be waitin' in 'is room. 'E sent me to fetch you."

"I'll get my cloak," Cornelia said.

" 'E said as you should come with me quick-like," the chambermaid said nervously.

"Very well, I will," Cornelia assented, guessing that Lord Furneaux was worried about Belinda's state of mind. She came out of the chamber and followed the girl down the hall. Then, as she stopped in front of a door at the far end of the corridor and knocked, Cornelia said, "But I thought his lordship was on the third floor."

"No, milady, 'e's 'ere," the chambermaid said with a slight smile.

The door was hastily opened, and much to her surprise, Cornelia found herself facing the unprepossessing man she had glimpsed below. She moved back hastily. "Who are you?" she demanded angrily. "And what is the meaning of this?" She looked around for the chambermaid and saw her staring triumphantly at the man, her hand held out.

"The meaning's that I wanted a second look at you, my love." He moved forward, and putting a hand on her arm, he pulled her roughly inside and threw a coin at the chambermaid as he closed the door.

"No!" Cornelia tried to reach the doorknob, but he stood in front of that portal, an ugly smile on his face. "Yes, you are beautiful." He grinned. "Damned beautiful. Thought so when I saw you downstairs. Damned if he should have you both."

Cornelia tried to pull away from him. "I . . . I think you must be f-foxed, my good man," she said furiously. "Now I will thank you to let me go!"

"Mayhap I'll let you go, my beautiful, come morning, and with a crown for payment. It's a goodly sum, but worth it, I think. Meanwhile . . ." He grinned.

"You will let me go immediately!" Cornelia cried. "I am here with my uncle and—"

"He's your uncle like I'm your uncle." He laughed coarsely. "And like that little redhead's your sister. He's welcome to her. I prefer you . . . my beautiful. Always had a hankering for golden-haired girls. And particularly a golden beauty like you. Now, give Dick Beaver a kiss, my love."

In that moment, Cornelia, vainly struggling against his strong and hurtful clutch, saw a candle in a brass holder on a table nearby. "Ohhh, oh, God," she screamed. "Are there two of you, then." She looked over his shoulder. "Oh, no, not two . . ."

"Two of me . . . what do you mean?" He looked away, his hold loosening, and in that moment Cornelia lunged for the candle holder and in one fluid movement struck him over the head. Screaming with rage and pain, he staggered back, and Cornelia, dashing to the door, was out and up the stairs to the third floor in seconds.

"Damn you, you . . ." She heard stumbling footsteps on the stairs back of her, and then, as she looked at a row of doors, she remembered that Lord Furneaux had told her that his room was above their own. She ran to the door in the middle of the corridor, frantically pounding on it as her would-be attacker came staggering up the stairs.

Had she found the right door? She could not be sure. "Lord Furneaux . . . Lord Furneaux . . ." she cried, wondering fearfully now if he were there. Had she mistaken the room?

The door was pulled open and Lord Furneaux, clad in a long brocade dressing gown, stared at her in amazement and a dawning concern. "Cornelia. . . what is amiss, my dear?"

"P-please . . ." She clutched his arm. "That . . . that man . . . D-Dick Beaver, he . . ." she half-sobbed, as she threw a terrified glance over her shoulder. "He tried to . . ." Her hand flew to her mouth as she heard pounding footsteps on the stairs and the sound of muttered curses. "He tried to . . ."

"Say no more, my dear, I understand." Lord Furneaux flung an arm around her shoulders, and pushing the door back, hurried her into his chamber. Then, coming out, he closed the door and stood against it as her furious assailant, having reached the top of the stairs, staggered toward him.

"Where is she . . . that damned . . ." He glared at Lord Furneaux. "Where's yer whore?"

Lord Furneaux fastened an icy stare on Mr. Beaver's face. "What is the meaning of this?" he demanded.

"Yon doxy . . ." the latter began. "She . . . she—"

"That is enough." Clenching his hand into a fist, Lord Furneaux struck him a powerful blow to the chin, sending him unconscious to the floor. In another second he had pushed back his door and dragged Mr. Beaver inside. Removing the belt of his dressing gown, he knelt beside the unconscious man and hastily bound his hands behind his back.

Rising swiftly, he turned to look at Cornelia, and found her standing near the window, her eyes wide and her face pale, but withal calm. "I think," he said breathlessly, "that we must leave this hostelry as soon as we may, my dear. I do not know about the . . . er . . . social standing Mr. Beaver enjoys here, but in the event that he is a good customer, I find that I do not care to remain under a roof that houses such a clientele."

She cast a nervous glance toward the window. "The weather . . ." she protested.

"Do you not believe that the weather is preferable to his company, my dear?"

A tremulous smile appeared and disappeared as she said, "I do, my lord. I definitely do."

"You can even smile," he commented wonderingly. "And you do seem remarkably calm despite what I imagine to have been a most unsettling experience, which you will explain in more detail once we are in the coach. I will dress, and you will please inform Belinda of the change in plans. I hope that this is agreeable?"

"It is, my lord," she said with just the suspicion of a quaver in her tone. "I will go at once."

"One moment more, my dear. I take it that the welt on this gentleman's head was not self-inflicted?"

"No, my lord, I inflicted it, and with a candle holder. Brass," she explained.

He smiled. "I can see that you are a female of infinite resources, and I must tell you that I am not surprised. I had already formed that opinion. I also find myself quite anxious to hear the rest of the tale."

"I will be glad to tell it to you, sir, but as you have said, I think it must be in the coach." She managed a smile and then hurried down the stairs to join Belinda, while his lordship went back to administer to the still-somnolent Mr. Beaver—the which included a gag in his mouth, a rope around his ankles, and a new berth—under the bed. After these hasty attentions, he dressed and went down to speak to his coachman.

The coach was going at a steady pace and over a road that was now familiar to Belinda. She was mentioning various landmarks to Cornelia, but while her friend nodded, she was still annoyed with her and had remained annoyed ever since she had mentioned the note she had left for Gerald. Of course, Cornelia had other things on her mind—namely her disturbing experience with that horrid Mr. Beaver, but oddly, that had not disturbed her as much as Belinda's confidence about the note.

Cornelia appeared to believe that the note was a direct invitation to Gerald and that he would be following them and might even have an angry confrontation with Lord Furneaux! Cornelia had suggested that he might even try to challenge his lordship. That, of course, was utterly ridiculous. Gerald would not pursue them! He would be relieved that she was gone, and if he were to do any pursuing, it would be in the direction of his adored Felice's studio! However, if by some outside chance he did insist on a confrontation with Lord Furneaux, the latter could certainly handle himself. In fact, Cornelia was far too concerned over his lordship. To her mind, she was making a grave mistake by speaking to him in what might be called a . . . familiar way.

As Belinda had told Cornelia, it did not do to become too interested in his lordship. In the years since his wife's death, many a female had cast out lures, to no avail. Her new friend Lady Evelyn had once likened him to an eel, saying that he was equally slippery. And she, for one, could see no difference in his attitude toward Cornelia at present than before she had come knocking on his door at the inn. He did occasionally ride back to point out one or another landmark, but his attitude toward them both remained as detached as ever.

"I do wish you had not left that note for Gerald," Cornelia suddenly said.

Belinda tensed. "I have told you, Cornelia, that I do not believe he will follow us—not when he can be with his mistress and—"

"And I have told you," Cornelia retorted crossly, "that you are refining far too much upon that situation. It is my belief that he has no interest at all in that woman, and if he were to catch up with us, he might call Lord Furneaux out. That would be poor thanks for all his kindness to you."

Belinda winced. "He was not due home until the day after we left," she said edgily. Meeting Cornelia's eyes, she added, "Very well, I . . . I, too, wish I had not left it for him. I do not know why I did. No, that is not quite true. I was angry with him. You must admit that I had a right to be angry with him."

"Yes, I will admit that, but if someone were going out of his way to do me a favor, I would not have deliberately put him at risk."

"I did not think of it that way. I only thought . . ." Belinda's eyes filled with tears. "I . . . I wanted Gerald to know what I thought. I suppose it was unwise of me." She swallowed a sudden lump in her throat as she remembered some part of what she had written. Had she suggested that her decision to leave with Lord Furneaux was based on her "high regard" for him? She had, she knew, and furthermore, she had underlined "high regard," which certainly she ought not to have

done. It might suggest to Gerald that that
"high regard" might carry with it an even
higher and warmer regard. Still, she was probably borrowing trouble. Gerald, finding her
gone, would not follow her. He would go joyfully to Felice, whose miniature he had placed
in a book of love poems! She blinked angrily
because of the increasing wetness in her eyes.
She would not, would not, *would not* weep
over his defection. She would put him out of
her mind!

"Oh, look," Cornelia suddenly exclaimed.
"There is the tower of the cathedral!"

Belinda turned to gaze out of the window
on Cornelia's side of the coach. Despite her
misery, she did thrill to the sight of the immense spire, seemingly touching the breeze-
driven clouds that floated above it. "Salisbury
Cathedral," she murmured. "Oh, it is beautiful. I wish we might stop to see it."

"I would like to visit the cathedral myself."
Cornelia nodded. "But I do not believe it safe."

"Why do we not ask Lord Furneaux what
he thinks?" Belinda asked.

"He did mention something about stopping
there, now that I remember it," Cornelia said.

"Well, if he approve the excursion, why
should we protest?" Belinda said reasonably,
the while she wondered why he had not mentioned such an excursion to her. He must
have spoken to Cornelia about it last night
after they arrived at the inn. She suddenly
recalled that Cornelia had not joined her in
the room they shared. Mary had remarked
upon it too, wondering where Lady Cornelia

had gone. She had not arrived until some twenty minutes later, and she had seemed a bit flurried when she entered the chamber. Had she been detained by Lord Furneaux? And if she had, what did it matter? He could not really be interested in a girl young enough to be his daughter, she thought resentfully.

That untoward resentment vanished swiftly. She had, she realized ashamedly, no reason to feel that Cornelia was her rival for the affections of a man who was merely trying to do her a kindness, and, quite truthfully, Cornelia was part of that same kindness—because Lord Furneaux thought she needed a chaperone. Still, the sooner Cornelia realized that he was interested in neither of them, the better it would be. She was not willing to acquit Cornelia of a penchant for him. A vision of that night they had seen him at Vauxhall arose in her mind's eye. Obviously that ballet dancer had been his mistress, just as the miniaturist performed that service for Gerald. Wives were not for loving. They were married for their dowries and their ancestry. She had brought both to Gerald, and before Lord Furneaux's wife died, she had obligingly presented him with a son. Were she, Belinda, to have a son . . . But she would not, she thought angrily. Gerald would have to have a son with his next wife . . . the one he would have to marry after the divorce, if he could bring himself to separate from his mistress . . . but he would not have to separate from her . . . She blinked and was extremely annoyed to find her ears filled with tears.

The cathedral was magnificent. Its spire, stretching up four hundred and four feet, seemed almost to reach the clouds, and though hundreds of years had passed since the edifice had been completed, the centuries had treated its intricate stonework very lightly. The only parts that showed wear were the battered faces of the statues rising on its western facade, but still the artistry of the conception remained.

Inside, there were paintings and sculptures, which were in a far better state of preservation. There were also effigies, and there was the splendid tomb of William Longspee, Earl of Salisbury and half-brother to King John. He had been laid to rest there in 1226, the first noble to be buried in the edifice.

Belinda was both impressed and depressed by these ancient tombs. Seen in the context of six hundred years, they made her feel small and insignificant, dwarfed by history, reduced to the size of an insect by the weight of past centuries and centuries to come. She felt a need to express this feeling to Cornelia, but somewhat to her annoyance, she found her friend talking to Lord Furneaux; or, rather, he was talking to *her*, smiling down at her and explaining something, for he was pointing to a tomb on which a figure lay, its feet on a crouching dog. She started toward them, her own observations demanding utterance, but there was something in the rapt gaze that Cornelia had fastened on Lord Furneaux's face that silenced her.

Once more she regretted Cornelia's pres-

ence on this journey and once more she was
heartily ashamed of herself for feelings she
had no right to entertain. Still, she did have
half a mind to confide Lady Evelyn's observations concerning his lordship in her friend's
ear, but she decided against it. Cornelia evidently enjoyed his company and undoubtedly
she was just as aware as herself of his disin-
terested kindness; after all she was some sixteen months her senior and that meant she
was sixteen months wiser in the way of the
Polite World.

They stayed that night in Salisbury and
left the town the following morning, taking
the road that must eventually bring them to
Taunton and thence to the stretch of land
that lay outside the village of Dunster, within
sight of the castle and having on it a shattered tower, once part of Devereux Castle. In
common with many such properties, it had
been leveled by the Puritans, but the house
that had risen in its stead was beautiful
enough. Still, Belinda, mulling over this ancient history, was discovering within herself
a great reluctance to return to her family
seat. She had adored it as a child, but faced
with the fact that she would probably spend
the rest of her life within its confines, she felt
a coldness around her heart and wished wildly
that she had remained in London.

Unfortunately, it was far too late for such
wishes. As her grandmother was fond of
saying, she had made her bed, and in another twenty-four hours she would be lying
in it, staring out at the stretch of garden that

lay beneath her window. She had seen it all her life and now she would continue to see it throughout all the myriads of seasons which would follow one the next until her death.

Closing her eyes, she leaned against the backrest. The road was smoother here, and consequently there was considerably less jolting. She ceased to clutch the strap at her side and folded her hands in her lap, staring moodily out at the passing countryside and wishing strongly . . . But she would not allow those threatening wishes to enter her consciousness!

She was not sorry that she had left Gerald and London behind. She did not wish to see either again, not ever! She would be happy in the country and she could also make herself useful. She would join her mother in improving the lot of their poorer tenants. She would also try to make her mother's life happier in other ways. They had a great deal in common. Both of them loved men who did not love them, who had visited their love on mistresses. Of course, she was more fortunate than her mother. She had not borne children. She had not gratified her husband by presenting him with the heir he must covet— but would never have from her! And it would not be easy for him to obtain a divorce . . . and . . . Her thoughts suddenly dispersed as, with a lurch, the coach came to a sudden stop, catapulting her to the floor.

"Belinda!" Cornelia cried, looking worriedly down at her. "Did you hurt yourself, my dear?"

"N-no, I . . . I do not b-believe so," Belinda replied confusedly. "Wh-what happened?"

"I do not know . . . some obstruction ahead. I cannot see from the side. . . . Give me your hand, my dear." Still clinging to the strap, Cornelia stretched her free hand toward Belinda, who, clutching it, was able to clamber back on the seat. "Are you sure you did not hurt yourself?" Cornelia inquired anxiously.

Belinda shook her head. "No . . . but . . ." She stared out of the window and was in time to see Lord Furneaux urging his horse into a canter as he passed them. He was frowning, she noted. A second later, she heard the sound of angry voices, one of which she recognized. She turned amazed eyes on a paling Cornelia. "It . . . it is Gerald and . . ." She came to a startled stop as she found herself addressing the air. Cornelia had opened the coach door and leapt to the ground. Following her, Belinda was in time to see an angry Gerald leading his horse as he advanced on Lord Furneaux, who had also dismounted.

"Stop him!" Cornelia cried to no one in particular.

"You . . . why . . . why are you here?" Belinda said confusedly as Gerald faced Lord Furneaux, glaring at him, the while the latter looked back at him, seemingly quite unperturbed at the sight of the angry or, rather, furious young man facing him.

"I bid you welcome, Gerald," he said coolly. "I might add that I expected you earlier, but perhaps you had trouble finding us?"

"Damn you for an unmitigated scoundrel!"

Gerald yelled. "Where is she? Where . . . ? What have you done with my wife, you damned roué? . . . God in heaven, you are old enough to . . . to be her father!"

Cornelia turned to Belinda, saying angrily, "Your note . . . see what you have wrought with your ridiculous note?"

Belinda did not so much as look at her. She was staring incredulously at her husband. "How did you . . . and why . . . ?" she blurted.

"My dear Gerald," Lord Furneaux said calmly, "your wife has sustained no harm at my hands. On the contrary, I quite expected that you . . ." He paused as the sound of hooves coming up the road at what appeared to be breakneck speed caused him to shift his gaze to a spot over Gerald's head and to say calmly still, but with an edge of surprise to his tone, "Ah, are we to entertain another firebrand, then? Or is he just a traveler on the way to . . . No, I rather doubt that. And what, pray, is his errand?"

"What are you talking about, and where is she?" Gerald suddenly broke off, seeing a man mounted on a huge black horse. He paled slightly. "The black horse," he said. "Death on a black horse . . ."

"What?" Lord Furneaux demanded.

As the horseman passed Belinda, she saw that he, too, had been riding swiftly. The sides of his mount were white with sweat. He reined in his mount and in one fluid movement dismounted.

To Belinda's utter amazement and subse-

quent confusion, she recognized Chrétien! A
spate of questions rose to her lips and fell
back into silence as the artist, lifting a long
bundle from his saddlebag, strode toward Gerald, dropping his burden at his feet. It fell
with a clang of metal. Then, stripping off his
gauntlets, he struck Gerald across the face,
saying furiously, "You will give me satisfaction, rogue. Here are swords." He pointed to
the bundle.

A hand to his assaulted cheek, Gerald regarded him in black amazement, which, in
that same moment, turned to utter fury. Dou-
bling his fist, he struck his would-be oppo-
nent on the chin, sending him staggering
back. "I do not cross swords with artisans
and knaves," he said contemptuously. "I use
a horsewhip, rather." Turning his back on
Chrétien, he stared at Lord Furneaux, saying
threateningly, "I do not want to ask you again.
What have you done with my wife?"

"Canaille!" Chrétien, leaping to his feet,
grabbed Gerald by the arm, and whirling him
around, said icily, "I am a duke in my own
right." He stretched out his hand, upon which
a golden ring gleamed. "This ring bears the
arms of my house, and if you do not choose
to fight me, I will gladly cut your damned heart
out for what you have done to the little Belinda
and to Mademoiselle D'Aubigny as well!"

"Very well, then." Gerald glared back at him.
"I have a score to settle with you too. You
with your devil's tricks . . ."

Cornelia ran to Lord Furneaux, crying frantically, "Stop them, I beg you will stop them."

He smiled down at her, saying calmly, "But why should I do that, my dear? I find this all very entertaining and even informative. However, it is not quite informative enough. I cannot quite understand why this man, whom I know to be an artist—he having painted one Lady Brindsley, and with remarkable fidelity, too—has joined us. And who was it told Gerald about our plans? I bowed to your advice and did not send the missive."

"Belinda left a note," Cornelia sighed. "I have been hoping against hope—"

"Alas, my dear," he interrupted with an ironic smile, "your hopes have proved futile, which was preordained, I must believe. And where, I wonder, does our friend the . . . er . . . duke fit in?"

"Please . . ." Cornelia threw a concerned and nervous look at the two angry young men. "They have their swords in hand. I beg you will stop them, my lord."

He shifted his gaze in that direction and in another moment had come to stand beside Gerald. "I beg you will sheathe your swords and try to behave rationally," he advised coolly.

"Rationally?" Gerald growled. "Be damned to you and your rationality . . . this miscreant, this nobody from nowhere, has filled my wife with a pack of damned lies and—"

"Do you call me a liar?" Chrétien demanded angrily. "I refute that. I will give you those lies down your throat."

"And I will slit your throat from ear to ear, you with your miniatures and your book of poetry." Gerald moved into a clearing and called to Chrétien, "*En garde*, Duc de Chiens!"

At Gerald's challenge, Belinda, who had been shocked and confused, suddenly came to her senses. "Nooo, nooo," she screamed. "Do not fight, I beg you will not fight!" She started toward them and was caught by Lord Furneaux as the furious pair of opponents crossed swords. She ran to Lord Furneaux, clutching his arm and crying wildly, "Stop them, stop them, oh, God, stop them!" Then, without waiting for his response, she ran toward the duelists and was summarily pulled back by Cornelia.

"It is too late, my dear!" she cried.

"Let me go . . . let me go!" Wrenching herself out of Cornelia's grasp, she came back to Lord Furneaux. "Oh, please . . . please stop them, my lord."

He shook his head, saying regretfully, "If it becomes necessary, I will stop them. However, I happen to believe that it is healthier if they exercise their anger in this way. Ah, *voilà!*" he exclaimed as the two young men locked blades, drew apart, and then circled each other, Gerald fighting with a dogged rush and Chrétien with a supple grave.

Belinda caught at Lord Furneaux's sleeve. "Please . . . please stop them," she said frantically. "There is nothing . . . nothing for them to fight about."

He said with just a trace of weariness, "Unfortunately, my dear, there rarely is."

She glared at him. "Why will you not stop

them?" she cried. "Can you not see that they mean to kill each other?"

"I doubt that, my dear," he said coolly. "A scratch or two and they will cease this madness of their own accord." He continued to watch them with a detached interest that served to further infuriate Belinda.

"You want them to hurt each other!" she accused him wildly. "To you it is just a sport. You do not care if either dies. You do not care."

"That is not true!" Cornelia came to her side. "You do not know him as I do, or you'd not spout such foolishness." She glanced at Lord Furneaux and found his eyes on her. She blushed, but continued insistently, "You are wrong, I assure you, Belinda."

Belinda glared at her. "And how is it that you understand Lord Furneaux so very well? He has been my friend nearly all my life and not just for a few spare minutes on the road."

Cornelia's eyes flashed. "Then I think you should realize that he is intrinsically kind and that he cherishes no animosity for either contender."

Belinda bridled. "Are you suggesting that . . . that—?"

"My dears," Lord Furneaux interposed hastily, "one duel at a time, I pray you."

A deep flush spread over Cornelia's face. "I am sorry," she apologized quickly. "I do not know what you must think of us."

He visited a long look on her face. "You must let me tell you one day, my dear, and that in the not-too-distant future." He glanced over her head and frowned, adding quickly, "I begin to think it were time I ended this skirmish. It is becoming far too ferocious and . . ." He paused, frowning and then strode forward hastily. "Damn, pinked!" he muttered, looking concernedly at the duelists.

" 'Pinked?' " Belinda, whose attention had been briefly deflected from the duelists, swiftly turned and, to her horror, saw blood staining Gerald's sleeve. He had not dropped his sword and he was still circling Chrétien, while the latter, a smile on his face, was obviously about to follow his advantage with another quick thrust. "No!" Belinda threw herself forward, standing in front of her husband, screaming, "No, no, do not dare to touch him, damn you! Can you not see that he is wounded?" She glared at Chrétien as Gerald quickly pushed her out of the way.

"My dearest," he cried hoarsely. "Are you mad? You might have been killed!"

"Belinda!" Cornelia had followed her, trying vainly to pull her away, while Chrétien, his sword falling from his suddenly nerveless grasp, stared at her in a consternation heavily laced with fury.

"*Tu es folle!*" he said gratingly. "*Tous les Anglais sont fous!*"

"My dearest Belinda!" Lord Furneaux had reached her side. He said gravely, "That was surely madness. I fear you do not know your own mind. If before we had started . . ." His eyes fell on Gerald, who had abruptly sunk to his knees. "Good God, lad!" he cried. Hurrying to Gerald's side and kneeling next to him, he slipped an arm around his shoulders, saying urgently, "Here, lad, let me help you. We must find a surgeon."

"No," Gerald weakly tried to push him away. "It is nothing! The merest scratch, I tell you." He looked up at Belinda. "My dearest, it is a lie . . . his lie . . . the artist."

She did not heed him. "It is much more than a scratch!" she cried fearfully, as she eyed the right sleeve of Gerald's shirt now turned crimson from the blood that also stained his hand and was soaking into the ground below him.

"He is bleeding so heavily!" Cornelia gasped.

"Nom d'un nom, un chirurgien, vite, vite," Chrétien cried.

"Yes, yes, a surgeon must be found and quickly," Lord Furneaux repeated.

"Come, I tell you it is nothing!" Gerald laughed and suddenly leapt to his feet. "You see!" he exclaimed triumphantly, and then, with an astounded look at no one in particular, he fainted, and were it not for Lord Furneaux's sudden move forward and for his strong, sustaining arm, Gerald must have fallen to the ground at his wife's feet.

8

The darkened chamber in a small hostelry called the King's Rest smelled strongly of mold. The furniture was battered and the sheets covering a narrow bed pushed against the wall were gray and much mended, but the man on that bed was unaware of the odor, or of the roughness of the sheets that covered him, or, in fact, of anything or anyone.

His face was hot with fever, and his gaze turned inward, staring at sights that were in his mind alone. In the last hour he had not stopped talking or, rather, babbling, and occasionally he started up, staring about him wildly. He was gently pushed back by the anxious young woman at his side, but he would not stop talking and he did not hear her anguished remonstrances. He had been in that condition ever since he had been carried up to the pair of rooms hired by Lord Furneaux. He had addressed several people, none of them visible, and sometimes he spoke of a huge black horse with flaming eyes, a horse that galloped through his dreams, bringing with it doom. However, at present the horse was gone and his words were audible and understandable as he painfully explained his feelings to the woman lurking behind his eyes.

"I did not know I would love her as much as I do, Felice. I am sorry to tell you this. We have been close, you and I . . . but this is different, it is different . . . Forgive me. Oh, God, why am I so warm? Felice, Felice, forgive me. I have treated you shabbily, but . . . but I did not know what love was until . . . I was with her and now she has left me . . . I have to find her. I have to tell her what is in my heart. Do you think she will believe me, Felice?"

"She will believe you, Gerald, my darling," Belinda said earnestly but futilely to his unhearing ears.

"She will not listen. She will not forgive," he groaned.

He had addressed her directly. He had looked at her as if he really saw her. Had he heard her? Had his fever finally diminished?

"Gerald . . ." She bent over the bed. "Do you know me, my love?"

He half-rose. "Damn you, Felice," he snarled. "I begin to think it was a plot . . . that painter. Did you pay him monies to make love to her? But no bribe would have been necessary. To look at her is to love her. And he is here . . . on his great black horse, Death on his horse . . . but I will kill him. He lied, Belinda, he lied with his miniature and his book . . . I never knew anything . . . about the book . . .

the library is a maze to me, and I never had her miniature." Anguish filled his tones. "I never had it, Belinda."

"I know that, Gerald, I know that now," she whispered.

"He lied," Gerald mumbled. "He lied . . . he lied."

"I know he lied," she sobbed. "Gerald, I know he lied," she said as loudly as she dared.

"Forgive me, please, please. . . ." He tried to raise himself, his eyes wide and blank. "Where are you, Belinda? Oh, God, she's gone. What am I to do?"

"Gerald," Belinda said urgently. "I am here. My love, I am here. Try not to toss and turn. You'll hurt yourself," she continued futilely, wishing that she could hold him down; but he was too strong for her and he would open the deep gash in his upper arm that had so narrowly missed an artery.

Behind her, the door opened, and after a few seconds, it closed. No one entered. Belinda was thankful for that. Poor Gerald would not want anyone to hear his feverish raving, herself least of all, she was sure.

And now, at least she knew the truth. Gerald loved her and her alone. She could not doubt that, could not doubt the truth of words spoken from the depths of a fever-stricken mind. Never again would she need to question his love for her. A shiver shook her. It was too high a price to pay for that truth.

"Oh, God, Gerald, oh, my darling, forgive me," she whispered. "I never thought to inflict such suffering upon you." She gently brushed a strand of sweat-soaked hair back from his forehead.

After looking into the sick man's chamber, Cornelia came down the narrow hall and carefully descended a winding stairway on which some of the treads were broken and the balustrade splintered.

In another moment she had entered the small common room, presently filled with passengers recently disembarked from a stagecoach. They were hurriedly eating the indifferent repast that would sustain them until the next stage, and casting curious and awed glances at a gentleman at a table near the back of the room. Though she was not in a smiling mood, such an expression quivered on her lips as she hurried toward Lord Furneaux. He looked, she thought, entirely out of place, a swan among ducks or, more to the point, a king among his humbler subjects. Reaching the table, she sat down.

He said, "You were not long."

"I did not go inside," she explained. "I didn't think she wanted me there. He is still feverish, that much I could tell. I do hope that there will not be any complications."

"I beg you will not worry," he said quickly. "Gerald is a healthy young man, and though the wound was, unfortunately, quite deep, the doctor cleaned it thoroughly."

"Thanks to you," Cornelia said a little grimly. "I do not believe he would have been half so thorough had you not insisted. He looked at you very oddly when you insisted that he swab the wound with whiskey."

"Whiskey is a great cleanser or, should I say, spirits in general are. Unfortunately, not too many people are aware of that. I myself found it out only by accident. As for the bandages, they must be changed every four or five days. Infection must needs be avoided. Is Gerald in much pain, do you think?"

"He is delirious . . . so I am not quite sure what he feels, poor young man. It is well that Belinda acted when she did."

"Yes," he agreed soberly. "I was badly mistaken about their intentions. Such anger as they exhibited has long been a stranger to me." He visited a rueful smile on her. "My youthful fires are long banked. Were that not the case, I would have foreseen the danger and would have brought the duel to an end much sooner or, rather, not have let it take place. I could have stopped it, I believe."

"They might have listened to you," she said dubiously, "but they were very angry. I think the cause lay deeper than what appeared on the surface."

"You may very well be right," he agreed.

"At any rate, it is well you were here, my lord," she said shyly. "You acted so quickly."

"Not quickly enough," he insisted. "And if I had not been here, I have a strong feeling that none of this would have happened."

She regarded him in blank surprise. "You surely cannot blame yourself for their quarrel."

"I should not have taken Belinda out of town." He frowned. "I am much older than she . . . I was not aware of the construction that Gerald must have placed on that." He sighed. "And I have always prided myself on being a reasonably accurate judge of character, but in this instance I certainly erred, and more than once." He stared at her fixedly. "But," he added, "I am not sorry for our journey out of London. I was definitely at loose ends, my dear. I needed a purpose. I needed a destination. I needed to rethink my life, and because of Belinda, I received considerable enlightenment."

"But at what cost . . ." she murmured.

"The cost was minimal, my dear Cornelia. For the past two days I have been comparing myself to a diver who goes looking for oysters to serve at a great feast and, lo, when he opens the shells, he finds a pearl of great price in one of them. It has been my great fortune to find a pearl that is, in fact, priceless."

She regarded him confusedly. "You are speaking in parables, I believe."

"You are quite right." He smiled. "And would you care to furnish an intepretation of this particular parable for me, my dear?"

"I am not sure that I could." She looked up at him, but unfortunately, his face was in shadow and she could not read his expression. However, she had a feeling that he was teasing her. He had to be teasing her. She had no right to entertain the foolish, foolish hopes that his semi-parable had aroused in her mind. All that she had heard about him from Lady Elizabeth, Belinda, and others of her acquaintance gave the lie to that.

"Would you care to have me interpret my parable for you?" he asked softly. "I should be glad to do so."

She said hesitantly and shyly, "I . . . I think you must, my lord. I find . . ." She paused, looking up in surprise as Chrétien suddenly strode to the table. A deep frown creased his forehead and was mirrored in his eyes. "Oh, dear," she murmured.

"What is it . . . ?" Lord Furneaux began, and paused as Chrétien reached the table. "Ah, Monsieur de Beaufort. You look as if you had weighty matters on your mind," he drawled.

Chrétien stared down at him, his expression enigmatic now. "I hope I may speak to you, my lord."

Cornelia started to rise. "I will leave you."

"No," Lord Furneaux said quickly. "I beg you will stay where you are, my dear. I am sure that you may hear what Monsieur de Beaufort wishes to say to me. Or do you wish that our conversation be private, monsieur?" He glanced up at the artist.

"No," Chrétien rasped. "It is not necessary. I wish only to know if you have spoken to a constable?"

Lord Furneaux raised an inquisitive eyebrow. "Should I have, Monsieur de Beaufort?"

"Is it not required?"

"It might be, Monsieur de Beaufort, but you see, I have not inquired as to what might be required. I take it that your journey has ended and you are eager now to return to London?"

Chrétien nodded. "Yes, my journey has indeed ended and I am extremely eager to return. Since I have chased the wild goose and lost my quarry, there is little reason for me to remain. I may leave, then?"

"If I were Hamlet, I would say that your departure would be a 'consummation devoutly to be wish'd,' monsieur. And do remember that I am quoting from Shakespeare and be kind enough to keep your sword arm at your side."

Chrétien laughed. "I would not dream of calling you out, Lord Furneaux. If we were, however, friends, I think I should enjoy a fencing match with you. I have a feeling that you would be my equal."

"If we were friends, I am sure I would enjoy such a match myself, Monsieur de Beaufort," Lord Furneaux said coolly. "Please do go, and in good health. If there are inquiries, I will explain that you had a commission in London."

"Ah, an admirable excuse." Chrétien turned to Cornelia. "Your servant, milady." He looked back at Lord Furneaux. "Your servant, my lord." He bowed.

"Your servant, monsieur," Lord Furneaux replied, keeping his seat.

As Chrétien strode out, Cornelia, watching him go, was extremely pleased that the conversation had not lasted any longer. She was even more pleased that the simmering anger she had divined in both men had not bubbled to the surface. However, before she could devote any more thought to that, Belinda, looking weary, yet far less strained than when she had accompanied her stricken husband to his chamber, came in.

"My dear," Cornelia said anxiously, "I do hope he is feeling better."

Belinda nodded. "Yes, he is. He does not seem to be in as much pain."

"I hope he is sleeping. He will require a great deal of sleep for the time being," Lord Furneaux said.

"He is sleeping," Belinda corroborated. She looked at him with a mixture of gratitude and embarrassment. "I . . . I am much in your debt, Anthony . . . I mean to say that *we* are. It was so kind of you to arrange for his chamber and for the doctor. You will certainly be recompensed once we have returned to London."

He said gently, "I beg you will not concern yourself with that, my dear Belinda. It is a sum hardly worth the words you have expended on it."

"Oh, no, no, I could not accept that," she said hastily. She flushed. "If only I had waited for an explanation. If . . . if I had not just blindly thrown myself on your mercy . . ."—she turned to Cornelia—"and on yours too, my dear, none of this would have happened and poor Gerald would not have been so hurt." Tears filled her eyes. "I . . . I have been so foolish." More tears arose and, brimming over, rolled down her cheeks. She brushed them aside with a shaking hand.

"My dearest," Cornelia said anxiously, "you are distraught and you are certainly not thinking clearly. You must go to bed. I will stay with Gerald."

"Oh, no, I could not let you do that." Belinda shook her head. "It is too much to ask, and besides, were he to wake, he would want me with him."

"But, my dear—" Cornelia began.

"I think that Belinda is quite correct in her assumptions," Lord Furneaux said. "I will have another bed moved into Gerald's chamber. And you . . ." He turned to Cornelia. "You are looking weary too. I think it were best if you retired for the night as well."

Cornelia was conscious of a disappointment so strong that tears threatened. From what he had been saying earlier, she had hoped . . . But obviously those hopes had no foundation in reality. She said, "I am rather weary. I will take your advice." She turned to Belinda, adding, "I am sure that Gerald will be the better for sleep, my dear. After all, no vital part was pierced."

"Yes, that is true." Belinda brightened. Then she sighed. "But it was all so useless." She turned to Lord Furneaux. "Good night, Anthony, and thank you again."

"It is nothing." He smiled. "Good night, my dear."

As Belinda hurried away, Cornelia said, "I will bid you good night too, my lord." She held out her hand.

He took her hand, and holding it warmly, brought it to his lips. Then, still holding it, he raised his head to say, "But wait here for a moment, will you? I must give some in-

structions to my man, but I will return as
soon as possible."

"Very well," Cornelia said on a breath. Obe-
diently she sat down in an adjacent chair,
but found herself far too restless to remain in
that position. Rising again, she moved rest-
lessly back and forth across the hallway, wondering what he wanted. Earlier she had hoped
. . . But her well-developed common sense told
her that such a hope was ridiculous. He was
not a man to tie himself down to one woman.
A vision of the beautiful little dancer who
had accompanied him to Vauxhall Gardens
on a night that seemed to be a hundred years
ago arose in her mind again. She also remembered what Belinda had told her concerning the wife, who had died so young, but
had left him an heir. He had no reason to
marry again. He . . .

"Ah, here you are!" Lord Furneaux came
striding quickly across the hall to stand beside her. Putting his arm around her, he
drew her against him. "My dear," he said
softly, gazing at her almost shyly, "there . . .
there is a great difference in our ages. You
are, I believe, no more than nineteen."

Cornelia gazed up at him, her heart in her
eyes. "I . . . I am not nineteen, my lord. I am
twenty," she murmured.

"Twenty . . ." He sighed. "That is very little
better. I am in my thirty-seventh year. Seven-
teen years stretch between us, but—"

"That is nothing," she dared to tell him.

He gazed at her eagerly. "Do you really believe that, Cornelia? When I am forty-seven—"

"I will be thirty, and I hope . . ." She paused, realizing that she was being far too bold.

"*I* hope that . . . Oh, Cornelia, I do love you," he said hoarsely. "I thought that I could never love again, but I was wrong. But, my dear, dear child—"

"I beg you will not call me a child," she said passionately. "I do not have a child's love for you and I believe you know that. I . . . I believe that you know how much I do care for you, my lord."

"Oh, my dearest, my beautiful," he said softly, brokenly, "I am not . . . I am never 'my lord' to you, never again. I am Anthony . . . and we must be married, you know. If I were to get a special license, we could be wed tomorrow. I wish it might be tonight, but tomorrow will have to suffice—or is that too soon for you?"

"If it could be accomplished within the instant, it would not be too soon, Anthony," she said passionately. "I . . . I do love you with all my heart." Her eyes filled with tears.

"And that is the way I love you, my beautiful," he said in a voice that was not entirely steady. He continued softly, "It is not a time for weeping, my dearest, my most beautiful and most practical angel. But it grows late, and you must go to bed—but also I want you to rise early, because I am afraid."

"You are afraid . . ." she said confusedly. "I do not understand."

He looked at her lovingly, one hand caressing her arm. "I am afraid that if I do not immediately pin you down with a marriage license, I will lose the woman I have come to love with every breath of my being."

"Oh, my lord, my dear, dear lord, you will never lose me," she said softly but fervently. "I will cling to you as ivy to a wall."

He laughed, albeit rather shakily. "How like you to speak in botanical terms. There are wide gardens on my estate . . . and you will have them at your disposal, my beautiful. But, Cornelia, dearest, you must learn one lesson, and that before we meet the minister on the morrow."

"What would that be?" she asked.

"You must continue to call me Anthony, else you will certainly confuse the poor man. I am sure he will not expect my fiancée to address me as 'my lord.' "

She laughed softly. "I will do my utter best to be letter-perfect on the morrow, Anthony."

"Oh, Cornelia, Cornelia, my good angel," he said huskily, and pulling her into his arm, he kissed her in the most satisfying manner possible.

It was a gray day in London. Tiny crystalline beads of mist coated the windowpanes, and the sun was merely a lighter glow in the leaden sky.

Felice, gazing out of her window, grimaced. The weather, heavy and hot despite the threatening rain, oppressed her. Still, it was no gloomier than the mood that had been with her when she awakened. She ran paint-stained fingers through her hair and then tensed. Moving swiftly to the door, she opened it, peering nervously into the hall.

"I thought I heard . . ." she muttered to herself, as, closing the door, she sighed and came back, sinking down on her couch and wishing she could rid herself of the tormenting fears and of the equally tormenting images that an all-too-vivid imagination was providing. There were pictures forming in the darkness behind her eyes, ugly, distorted pictures like those imagined and painted by Hieronymus Bosch—fragmented bodies, demonic faces. In the midst of these mind-conjured terrors, there came a tap at her door, the door that she might have left on the latch, she thought, and turned cold as the knock was repeated. She had left her door on the latch, she remembered. She grabbed a palette knife and rose to her feet as that portal quivered and then swung open. Felice reached it at the same time that a tall mud-splashed man entered and stood against the door, saying in French, "Had you intended to drive that knife into my bosom, my love?"

"Chrétien!" Felice cried in a mixture of relief and gladness. "Oh, Chrétien!" She threw her arms around him. "Oh, I was so afraid . . . but you are all right. You have not been hurt?"

He clasped her in his arms and kissed her with a passion that surprised her. When finally he raised his head, he said, "I am quite all right and I do thank you for your concern, my beautiful. I will add that I have—in some little measure—avenged you for the suffering you have recently endured."

She stiffened. "What do you mean?"

"I fear that your erstwhile lover—I speak of young Gerald Courtenay—"

"You have not killed him!" she cried fearfully. "Oh, Chrétien, you must not be seen here. They must not find you or—"

"*They* are not searching for me, my dearest. Of course I have not killed him. The penalties I would have to face for such an action would not be to my liking. I have given him only a gentle hint that I believe he will take to heart—a heart that is still beating strongly, my Felice. I did puncture him . . . but only in the arm, and his bride is tending him and he now knows that he should not have played fast and loose with your affections. They are far too precious for that."

"Oh, C-Chrétien," she stammered. "I . . . I do not know what to say."

"I hope that you will say that you love me, my dearest."

"But that you know already, my Chrétien." She saw him suddenly wavering in her tears.

"Yes, and though you might not be aware of it, I have treasured that love, even when my attention has been—shall we say?—diverted." He gave her a mischievous smile. Then he sobered, and staring down at her intently, continued, "I have very little to offer you, but do you love me enough to marry me?"

Happiness thrilled through her and then vanished as she stared up at him unhappily, realizing that the union he offered was impossible. She said sadly, reluctantly, "But, Chrétien, my dearest, you know you cannot marry me. Napoleon has suffered strong reverses. The allies might very well push him to the wall and—"

He laughed softly. "I did not ask you for your interpretations of current military activities, my dearest. I love you, Felice. I want you for my wife."

"But, Chrétien," she protested, "you are aware that Gerald was . . . was not the only one."

He nodded. "I know all about you." His voice deepened and grew oddly husky. "I know, too, that I want to marry you, and if the time comes that I am allowed to return to my estates in France, you must return with me. I am comfortable with you, my Felice. I am happy and I hope I am not wrong in saying that I believe you care for me also."

She gazed up at him, wondering if she were dreaming, but of course she was not dreaming. He was there, his arms about her, holding her a shade too tightly. She said breathlessly, "I more than care for you, Chrétien. I think you know that. I love you with all my heart, but I never believed—"

"Then, naturally, you must marry me," he said positively.

"Am I dreaming?" she whispered.

He said softly, "I think I must prove to you that you are not, my Felice, my wonderfully understanding, forgiving Felice. I think I must prove to you that this is reality." He removed

a gold signet ring from his finger and slipped
it onto her third finger, left hand. "With this
ring, I thee will wed . . . and on it you see the
quarterings of our house . . . our house, my
love, for if I receive back my title, you and
none other will be my duchess."

"Oh, Chrétien . . . I care nothing for titles.
I love you. I cannot remember a time when I
have not loved you more than life."

Sunshine crept through the curtains of the
chamber and spilled a ray on the face of the
girl drowsing in a chair by the bed where her
husband had lain for the last two days.

The brightness failed to rouse her, but Gerald, blinking against that same brightness,
pulled himself up against the headboard of
his bed and winced at the sharp pain in his
arm. He wondered how he had come by it.
Then his eyes fell on the chair and widened.
He started to stretch out his hand, but stopped
quickly as more pain shot through his arm.
With the pain came memory in the form of a
set of images as vivid as the sunlight, passing swiftly before the eyes of his mind. Then,
once more, he gazed at the sleeping girl and
was confused—for here was Belinda, who had
been so angry with him . . . who had fled his
house . . . who had accused him of loving
Felice . . . and now she drowsed in the chair,
her face pale, dark shadows under her eyes,
and it seemed to him that he had heard her
voice in the night and . . .

In that moment Belinda opened her eyes.
She looked at the man on the bed and her

gaze sharpened. "Oh, dear, he's awake," she murmured half to herself. "I wonder how long . . . I must . . ."

"Belinda," he said softly.

She tensed and stared at him, saying hopefully, "Do . . . do you know me, then, Gerald?"

"Why would I not know you, my dearest?" he began confusedly. Then he frowned. "But . . . but you are angry. You believe—"

"No," she assured him hastily. "No, I know the truth." She blinked away a sudden rush of tears. "I was a fool not to have waited until you returned . . . but he told me—"

"I know what he told you, that damned artist, and it is all lies," he said passionately. "I swear to you—"

"Shhh, shhh, you must not allow yourself to be excited . . . you have been hurt, my dearest. And . . . and there is no need for you to swear, Gerald. I know the truth, and it is all my fault that you were wounded." More tears rose in her eyes. "How can you ever forgive me?"

"Oh, my own darling . . ." There were tears in his eyes too. "I do love you so much."

"And I love you with all my heart," she said happily.

"But, my Belinda, you are too far away," Gerald protested. "Come, lie beside me, my own."

"But your arm . . ." she protested.

"There is nothing the matter with my left arm . . . and beneath that arm is my heart. No," he contradicted as she slipped into bed beside him, "it is not."

"What are you saying, Gerald, love?" Belinda demanded confusedly.

"I am saying that *you* are my heart, my love."

"And you are mine," she murmured, and abandoned herself to an embrace that was loving, passionate, and eminently satisfactory, despite the fact that her husband had the use of only one arm.

EPILOGUE

The countess, becomingly garbed in a diaphonous green gown that matched her eyes and set off her admirably coiffed auburn hair, was curled in a large leather chair, reading from a closely written, somewhat blotted sheet of paper. Since she was nearing the end of her newest novel, there was a large pile of manuscript on the table beside her chair. Now, coming to a stop, she looked at the lady sitting across from her in another comfortable armchair.

"Cornelia," she began. "I wonder if . . ."

She received an annoyed glance. "Why did you stop reading, Belinda? We have not much time, and I am eager to hear the rest of it. You cannot leave me hanging in midair like this . . . to say nothing of your unfortunate heroine."

"Oh, dear Cornelia, I am sorry, but my attention was momentarily distracted by your gown."

"My gown? Is there something the matter with it?" Cornelia looked down anxiously.

"No, silly, nothing is the matter. I was thinking about my next book, the one I intend to write after I have heard what my publisher has to say about this one. I would like to describe your gown. I love the color. Purple becomes you, my dear and I intend that my heroine have gray eyes, too. In fact, I intend to describe you."

"I am flattered," Cornelia smiled. "How many volumes will I be?"

"At least five," Belinda said thoughtfully. "And ruffled at the hem."

Cornelia appeared understandably confused. "I am not sure I catch your meaning, my dear. How may a volume be ruffled at the hem?"

"Silly, I meant your gown." Belinda stared at the gown in question. "It seems simple, but I know it is not. Indeed, it is a miracle of the mantua maker's art. I expect it came from Paris, too?"

"Yes, it did," Cornelia acknowledged. "However, not all my gowns are made there, as you seem to imagine. And why, pray, are we discussing my gowns when I want to hear the end of your story? I really do love it."

"Indeed?" Belinda smiled beatifically. "You are always so kind, Cornelia."

"I think you know that I am not being kind, Belinda. I am honest. Believe me, I would tell you if I did not like your novel. You know that for a fact. But I happen to think that this one is quite your best."

"Are you suggesting that you did not like my last book?" Belinda inquired sharply.

"No, my dearest," Cornelia said patiently. "*The Lady of Oakridge Grange* was quite thrilling, but I do enjoy stories that take place in dark and gloomy castles with secret passages, ruined towers, and mad relatives. Please, Belinda, do finish reading!"

"Very well," the author responded rather edgily. "But I liked *The Lady of Oakridge Grange*. It *was* very well received you know."

"Yes, I do know." Cornelia stifled an annoyed click of her tongue. She continued carefully, "*The Lady of Oakridge Grange* deserved the great success it had. I told you that I liked it. I only said that I have a slight preference for gothic settings and you have written a truly lovely ruin. The bats gave me the shivers. But do go on reading, for they will soon be here and then we will have to be on our way to the reception."

"Very well." Belinda suddenly grinned. "I expect I am difficult. Gerald says I am. It is not that I do not appreciate criticism . . ."

"My love, say no more. No author appreciates criticism—even though it is a necessary evil." Cornelia rolled her eyes. "Pray continue, if you please. I would read it, myself, but I cannot fathom your scrawl."

"I do not understand why . . . but never mind," Belinda hastily turned her eyes back to the page and began to read. " 'The bride and groom had entered the ancient chapel while above them, the wind wailed eerily around the ancient edifice, blending ominously with the sounds swelling out of the great organ.

" 'Miranda, standing on the sill of that broken window, stared down at the pair and their attendants. Vagrant winds blew her ebony garments about her wasted form. Her thin face was deathly pale, and her eyes, sunk in great hollows, appeared like deep black wells as she watched Alfred and Ernestine joyfully walking toward the great altar.

" 'Clasping her hands, Miranda silently mouthed the dread spells she had filched from old Dame Alice before she had strangled the sorceress, once her mentor. She listened tensely to the ominous wail of the winds, precursors of the great storm which she, through her craft, had invoked. In seconds, it must come, must batter against the old walls, must shatter that glass yet remaining in the windows and hurl its razor-edged fragments down upon the hapless bridal pair. Yet, though she continued to mutter those arcane phrases, the winds suddenly died down and the brilliant sun emerged from behind a cloud.

" 'The ancient minister spoke the beautiful words that united the happy lovers and then the bride's attendant lifted her lacy veil and a blissful Alfred pressed a long kiss on Ernestine's lips.

" 'Uttering a long, piercing shriek, Miranda flung herself from the window and was dashed to pieces on the jagged rocks at the foot of the castle.' That is the end," the author said with no little satisfaction.

"Oh, dear, poor Miranda." Cornelia sighed. She received a most indignant glance from the author. "You cannot be telling me that you feel *sorry* for Miranda, Cornelia. Certainly she met a deserved death. Just think, her evil machinations kept the poor lovers apart for fully five years!"

"Indeed, they did. You are very ingenious, my dear. Those were five very interesting years, and each time I was positive that Alfred and Ernestine would get back together, Miranda came up with yet another fiendish maneuver. I adore the way you described the banshees, the ghosts, the escaped python and Miranda's horrid potions, not to mention her confrontation with the devil!"

"I hope that you found it mysterious enough."

"Oh, I found it deliciously mysterious, though the far greater mystery to me is how you manage to find the time to write such long novels, between traveling to Rome two years ago, France last year, and the coronation and taking care of two children . . . it is nothing short of miraculous! When do you expect this book to be published?"

"Well, Mr. Babcock will have to read it first."

"He will love it, I assure you. It is quite your best."

"I hope you are right," Belinda said thoughtfully. "I do not want to do any rewriting unless it is absolutely necessary, mainly because I have an idea that will take us to Spain this summer."

"Spain? Oh, lovely. Would you be planning a modern romance, based on Wellington's victories—of course, I mean a member of his staff and a señorita."

"Ummmm," Belinda said thoughtfully, "it is not a bad idea. However, in common with Sir Walter Scott, I prefer the past when it comes to novels. I hope to write the tale of a Moorish princess and a Christian knight. It will be set in Granada, and I believe I will use some historical characters this time."

"Oh, lovely!" Cornelia exclaimed. "If I had any talent for writing, I think I would like to write about the French Revolution. But, unfortunately, I do not have any talent."

"You do have a talent for designing gardens, my dear. Aunt Elizabeth never stops singing your praises. And you are a wonderful mother, not to mention stepmother. Jasper loves you just as much as little Helena and Elizabeth do. They are so adorable, your twins."

"I wish I could have more children." Cornelia sighed.

"Do not even think of it," Belinda said anxiously.

"It would do no good to think about it," Cornelia said ruefully. "The physician tells me that I cannot conceive again."

"I am sure your husband will not repine."

"No." Cornelia smiled. "He adores the girls and he insists that three children are quite enough."

"And three such happy children . . ." Belinda began, and paused as she heard the clock chime. "Gracious, it is almost time to leave. I wonder where our husbands have gone? They said they would meet us here. I expect they are discussing the present government. I hope they remember that we are due at that reception and ball given by the Duke and Duchess de Villars. I am quite dying to attend—are not you?"

"I must say that I am," Cornelia nodded. "I understand that it is something of a miracle to receive a card."

"I have heard that, myself." Belinda turned wide eyes on her friend. "How do you imagine that we both received invitations to that ball? They are intimates of Louis XVIII and all the *ton* is babbling of their extravagance. Imagine to have leased a whole house just for the ball and the supper afterward! I vow I can hardly wait to meet them."

"I am of your mind," Cornelia smiled. "I have heard that the duke comes from an ancient family and is extremely wealthy. Of course, he was banished after the fall of the monarchy and narrowly escaped execution. He is reputed to have lived in Italy and Switzerland."

"And the duchess, I expect that she, too, suffered during the Revolution. The usual cabbage-cart situation, I imagine?"

"I beg you will not be so blasé, Belinda," Cornelia chided. "Those were terrible times. I am glad that the poor émigrés can return to something like their former splendor."

"I can think of one pair of émigrés for whom I do not feel especially sorry," Belinda remarked caustically. "The agony that rascal put poor Gerald through. He might easily have taken off his arm and I am sure that if Gerald had not turned when he did, he would have run him through the heart. I wanted to burn his portrait, but Gerald would not have it."

"I cannot blame him for that. It is a lovely piece of work and amazingly like you."

"I do not want it in this house! Whenever I think of Chrétien de Beaufort's wicked lies . . . and I do think of them every time I see his horrid portrait and—"

"My dear," Cornelia interrupted Belinda's burgeoning diatribe gently. "That all took place a very long time ago and really, it does not bear thinking about."

"No," Belinda visited a rueful smile on her friend's face. "You are right, of course. We ought not to be dwelling on matters so unpleasant when we are bound for a gala evening presided over by a mysterious duke and duchess who have seemingly sprung upon the London scene like mushrooms after a rainstorm."

"Or toadstools," Cornelia said.

"Now who's being unpleasant?" Belinda inquired lightly.

"I plead guilty." Cornelia grimaced. "I know that the French are our allies now, but still I cannot warm to them."

"Nor I," Belinda agreed. "But I expect that we had best reserve our judgment until we meet our host and hostess. I understand from Gerald that the family is an old one, so old, in fact, that they consider the Capets upstarts. I believe they are distantly related to Isabella D'Angoulême, who wed King John."

"And who was, I have read, no better than she should be," Cornelia commented. "King

John had one of her lovers hanged in her boudoir."

"Ah, well, that was a long time ago. Let us give them the benefit of the doubt," Belinda said tolerantly.

"Are you impressed?" Belinda murmured some two hours later as she and Cornelia preceded their husbands up a long flight of red-carpeted white marble steps where, at intervals, stood footmen in military uniforms of white and gold with touches of red. They wore powdered wigs and held themselves as stiffly as if they were on review before his majesty King George IV.

"The house is certainly grand," Cornelia murmured. "Though to my thinking, everything is just a little too grand, as if, indeed, they were determined to out-Carlton Carlton House."

"My feeling exactly. It is all rather excessive." That opinion received further bolstering as they came into the ballroom, a vast chamber magnificently decorated in gold and white. Huge baskets of roses were set between shining mirrors, the clarity of which pronounced them Venetian glass. They reflected a magnificent three-tiered crystal chandelier into infinity, and with it the numbers of distinguished guests already dancing to the music of a small orchestra discreetly hidden by an arrangement of screens.

A waltz was in progress and a glance assured Belinda that not only were there a great many members of the *ton* present, but also

Prince William, the king's eldest brother and heir.

"They certainly cannot be toadstools," she managed to murmur to Cornelia.

"What are you saying, my love?" Gerald asked.

"Nothing of any importance," she replied quickly.

Their host and hostess were, at the moment, surrounded by a group of guests who had come up the stairs ahead of them, but as these went on into the ballroom, the duke and duchess turned to greet the new arrivals.

They proved to be a handsome pair. The duke, tall and slim, and with only a few threads of gray in his dark hair, looked to be in his early forties. He was clad in the regulation black and white evening wear that nearly all gentlemen wore in deference to the dictates of Beau Brummell, even though the latter had been debt-banished to Calais some five years ago. A row of medals gleamed on the duke's chest and around his neck was the ancient Order of St. Michael, which had been reestablished after the fall of Napoleon. The duchess, serenely beautiful and dignified, wore a gown of golden silk which showed off a slim and lovely figure. Diamonds gleamed in her tiara, in a magnificent necklace, and in her long matching earrings.

They greeted their guests cordially, if not effusively, and received much the same greeting in return. Then, as the foursome came into the ballroom, Cornelia, exchanging a swift glance with Belinda, mouthed something before she moved into her husband's arms for a waltz.

Seeing Belinda nodding and smiling at her friend, Gerald asked curiously, "What was all that about, my dear?"

"Toadstools, my darling," she murmured.

"What can you mean?" He regarded her quizzically.

"I am thinking of incorporating it into the title of a book I am planning," she explained.

"Is that not rather an odd title for one of your books, my love?" he asked.

"It will be a rather odd book," she replied, smiling up at him, "but," she added thoughtfully, "I have a feeling that it will sell."